Two P's in a Pod

TWO P'S IN A POD

by Susan Terris

GREENWILLOW BOOKS

A DIVISION OF WILLIAM MORROW & COMPANY, INC.

NEW YORK

Title page illustration by Byron Barton

1 2 3 4 5 6 7 8 9 10

Library of Congress Cataloging in Publication Data
Terris, Susan. Two P's in a pod.
Summary: The new girl decides to make Pru a leader in
their sixth grade class and Pru enjoys her new
popularity until she realizes the importance
of being her own person.
[1. Friendship—Fiction.   2. School stories]   I. Title
PZ7.T276Tw   [Fic]   77-8488   ISBN 0-688-80107-2
ISBN 0-688-84107-4 lib. bdg.

For Amy and
all the other sixth graders I know,
who by the time this book is published
will be grown-up seventh or eighth graders
too old to admit
that these kinds of things
ever happen . . .

Two P's in a Pod

my ear interrupted

1.

"WHAT IF . . . ?" I WAS ASKING MYSELF AS I WATCHED Brooke, Alyson, and the others beginning to fall into a gaping crevasse that had just opened in the school-yard as the result of a sudden, violent earthquake. "What if . . . ?"

As I was doing my very best to finish the sentence and, at the same time, allow a dark, brooding, hand-some stranger to reach down from the back of his stallion and snatch me to safety, a voice very close to my ear interrupted.

"You know, I'm a leader, and *here* nobody knows it."

"Huh?" I said, using one of the elegant verbal expressions that always annoy my language-conscious mother. While I was saying "huh," I twisted myself around to see whether the person speaking was inside or outside my head.

Outside, I reassured myself, turning to look at the girl who had seated herself next to me on the fender of Mr. Harrington's 1958 two-tone green convertible. (A horrible-looking, old, full-of-chrome machine that he—my homeroom and English teacher—had been driving since eight years before I was born.)

The girl by my side spoke again, repeating for a second time exactly what she had already stated quite clearly before. "I said . . . I'm a leader, and nobody here even knows it! What's the matter with you, Pru? Are you deaf or something?"

"How do you know my name?" I demanded, scooting my blue-jeaned bottom a little farther away so I could get a better look at this girl whom I had *never* seen before.

"Well, I saw you sitting here on this hip old car so I asked who you were," she replied, giving me a strange, secretive smile.

I could feel myself frowning as I examined her. She had an unusual, snaky scarflike thing wound around her head. She was, as I already said, a complete and total stranger. But still, as I looked at her and felt five hundred and seventy-seven goose bumps playing leap-frog across my scalp, I knew that there was something terribly familiar about her.

"What's your favorite thing?" she asked me, as I was trying to figure out where I could have seen her before.

"Books," I answered, without even pausing to think.

"What kind?"

"Well . . . ," I began, "I used to like 'I' books. . . ."

"Eye books?" she interrupted, pointing up at her own bright green eyes.

I shook my head. "No, no—'I' books. You know, the ones that always begin with 'I want to tell you the story of my life,' like Judy Blume writes. But now I read only romantic books—like *Green Mansions* or *Jane Eyre* or *The Scarlet Letter*."

The girl nodded enthusiastically. "I like that, Pru," she said. "You must be a very unusual and distinctive person."

Encouraged by her words, I continued. "Yes, all those old novels with dark, handsome men and women in long skirts and dangling earrings and . . . ."

"Shall we pierce our ears?" she asked, not at all bothered by the fact that she was not only interrupting again but changing the subject, too.

Don't ask me why I did what I did next, but I did it. Instead of continuing to make pleasant conversation with someone who was quite obviously—on the first day of school after Christmas vacation—about to become a new student at Portola Hill School, as I'd been myself only a year and a half ago, I did something else. I reached out and pinched her. On her arm. Hard.

You see, I wasn't used to this kind of before-school chat. Nobody liked me at Portola Hill. Nobody important, at least. I had tried and tried to get Alyson and Brooke to like me but they didn't. They said I had a terrible temper—which I did, when they were insulting me—and that I was a bookworm and spent too much time what-iffing. Most of the time, no one talked to me unless they were saying things like "What pages are we supposed to do for English, Pru?" or "Pru, your pants are unzipped."

So when I reached out and pinched this reasonably friendly being who had asked my name and then come over to sit next to me on Harrington's fender, I was doing so just to make sure she actually existed.

"Ouch!" she cried out in a voice that was quite believably real. Then, before I could move or say a word, she pinched me back.

"Ouch," I echoed, suddenly aware that Portola Hill would never be as grim for me as it had been before this girl appeared—this girl who was still so strangely familiar.

Then, not at all offended that I'd pinched her and agreeably allowed her to return the pinch, she flashed me a smile. Her smile was so bright someone might have wanted to take a picture of it for a toothpaste commercial.

"I'm Penny," she said, beginning to unwind the rolled, gauzy headdress she was wearing. "Penny Hoffman. I was over at Anza—in the sixth grade there. I was a leader at Anza, but my folks moved at Christmas because my dad's got emphysema and can't climb steps. So now I'm here—here and a nobody, like you probably are, Pru—a nobody in Mr. Ronald Harrington's sixth-grade homeroom. I met Mrs. Monzoni, your principal. She said I'd like Mr. Harrington—that everybody does, whatever that means. Will I? Will I like him?"

This person named Penny had never met me and had already insulted me by assuming I was the nobody I really was, but instead of taking offense and turning away, I simply gave her a display of my own Ultra Brite teeth. Then, instead of answering her question about Harrington, I breathlessly began to tell her the story of my life. "I'm Pru—Pru Phillips. Prudence, but no one calls me that. Just Pru—except for Mom, who sometimes calls me Prudie or Prune. I'm twelve, sixty-seven pounds, green eyes, black hair. I've lived in Detroit, St. Louis, Atlanta, Pittsburgh—and now San Francisco. All the smoggy places because my father's in smog—an engineer, you know. We've been in all the smoggy places except Los Angeles. My father says he could work with Buddha, Moses, Matthew, Mark, Luke, John, and Ralph Nader and still not make any improvement in *their* smog. Now, Mom, she paints eggs —eggs with their insides blown out—but mostly she writes, or tries to. Articles about fish. Can you imagine —fish? She even belongs to a writers' group at the S.F. Library—the same one Mr. Harrington belongs to. Then, after Dad and Mom, there's my brother Lionel. He's nine, and terribly smart. We call him Lion, though, because . . . ."

"Shut up," Penny said. She said it without the least bit of insult or meanness. (Usually when someone tells me to shut up, I yell at them. Loud.) She was still smiling and unwinding her head as she said this to me. She let a waterfall of heavy, shining black hair spill down upon her shoulders and back. I shivered as I looked at it because it was very similar to the half-curly, unruly hair growing out of my own head.

"I'm sorry," I told her, wishing I hadn't let myself get so carried away.

"Don't be sorry. I want to know all that, Pru, really I do. There will be time later for those things. But, first things first—and quick, before the bell rings."

"What?" I asked, happily savoring her insistence that she and I were going to have all kinds of time for becoming friends, for exchanging all the special, important little details of our lives the way I used to do with Ruthie in Pittsburgh before we moved. "What if . . . ," I asked myself, "Penny is going to become the same special kind of . . . ?"

"Who is the most popular girl in the class?" Penny asked, interrupting my thoughts in a soft but business-like way.

As I answered, I watched with amazement as Penny took the coiled headdress and wrapped it around her waist until it formed a fashionable, twisty striped belt with two tasseled tails hanging down against her faded jeans.

"Brooke," I told her, pointing to where Brooke was laughing and holding court smack in the middle of the schoolyard. "And Alyson. Brooke Cole and Alyson Auerbach. They're best friends and they call themselves the Ladybugs. But they aren't very nice—either of them. At least, not to me."

Penny slid off the fender of the car. Then she reached back and pulled me down, too. "Fine—good," she said, linking her left arm through my right one. "Now tell me something else. Who is the weirdest, most unpopular girl in the class? The nerdiest nerd?"

"Me," I answered.

Penny laughed. "You? You're no nerd. Stop joking with me. Now tell—who is it?"

The answer was very simple, really. I was unpopular, but in comparison to Martha Brandeberry, I was utterly adored. If *her* pants had been unzipped, no one would have even bothered to tell her. But they wouldn't have been, because Martha never wore anything to school but a skirt. It was a green corduroy skirt, and she wore the same one every day. With a leotard and ballet slippers, but she didn't even *dance*. (Once, when I had just come to Portola Hill and didn't realize that no one talked to Martha, I had asked her.)

All I had to do was point a finger and Penny, squeezing my arm slightly, knew. "Martha Brandeberry," I whispered, seeing the same tall, full-chested sixth grader my new friend Penny was seeing. We both gazed at Martha, who was slumped against the railing next to the door, her shoulders hunched, her limp dishwater blond hair hanging close to her face the way her green skirt clung to her bare legs.

"Okay," Penny said, releasing my arm and springing forward like some exotic jungle cat. "That's where we start, you see—if you want to be at the *top*. If you want to be a leader, too, like I am!"

"Me, a leader?" I asked, laughing.

"Of course," Penny insisted. "Both of us. Why not?"

My head was spinning as I skipped to keep up with Penny Hoffman's swift gait and swinging black hair. "Wait—wait," I pleaded. "I don't understand. I'm sorry, but what are you talking about?"

"Stick with me, Pru. I'll show you. Just stick with me."

Although I still felt confused, I did exactly as she said. In the short five minutes before first bell, I dis-distracted Martha by asking her how far she'd gotten in *The Yearling*, which we were all reading for Harring-ton's English class. While I was listening to Martha's low, even voice tell me she'd finished last week and watching her examine my face trying to figure out why, after a year and a half, I'd finally decided to talk to her again, Penny silently stole her frayed orange book bag.

As Penny was hopping up the steps and into the dis-infectant-smelling school corridor, the first bell rang. "Got to go," I mumbled, abandoning Martha and fol-lowing light-fingered, light-footed Penny down toward the lockers. With only a little guidance from me, Martha's book bag was safely hidden in the bottom of

Brooke Cole's ladybug-stickered locker by the time the second bell clanged.

"Tell me about Harrington," Penny urged as we hurried away from the lockers and pushed along toward the stairway up to Homeroom #307.

"I can't. I can't," I protested, panting and laughing. "About *him*—you'll just have to find out for yourself."

Not only was I light-headed over having a friend and confused that *I'd* ever be one to take part in the kind of mean prank Brooke and Alyson usually played on other people, but I was out of breath from the quickness with which it had all taken place. Poor Martha. It was always *her* locker in which other people's stolen items were deposited. How could Penny know the first time she set foot in Portola Hill that nothing—absolutely nothing—could be more perfect that to reverse it all and make someone like Brooke, for once, look guilty?

We rushed, but still, because of our frantic, last-minute activity, we were late—the last ones in.

And there he stood, next to the desk—Mr. Ronald Harrington—tall, lean, and solemn-faced with his neatly trimmed graying hair and beard. In his room, I hated to be late, hated anything that called too much attention to myself, but today with Penny I knew it was going to be all right.

We had hardly run through the doorway, however, when the strangest murmur began to roll through the classroom. I had intended, with an unusual show of courage, to introduce Penny to Mr. Harrington, but suddenly I found myself stiff as a statue as the murmur swelled louder and louder.

The students were saying something over and over. They must have been speaking ordinary, jabbery sixth-grade English, but I couldn't seem to understand a word as I stood there, frozen, next to Penny.

At last, I heard one voice above the others, a deep boy-voice belonging to Cal Williams. I hated him—hated him because I always saw him peeing against trees in the park near our house.

"Alike! Alike!" he was yelling, for now the murmur had turned into an ear-splitting din. "Pru and that girl —they look just alike!"

Feeling one more shiver run through me, I turned to look at Penny, who was already looking at me with her bright, toothy smile. Familiar, I had thought to myself outside, strangely familiar. Now, before Home-room #307, we stood there facing one another. Two twelve-year-old sixth graders. About the same height and weight. Both thin. Both flat-chested. Both with green eyes and heads of long, thick, half-curly black hair. Quite alike except for our faces. My nose was smaller. Her mouth and chin were wider. Her eyebrows were more arched. But everything else, as Cal had shouted out, was alike in a wonderful but totally creepy way.

Harrington was banging and banging with his yardstick for some kind of reasonable silence. I was forcing myself to turn away and stop staring at this girl, who was not my sister, not my cousin, not any kind of even distant relative, and yet who looked like me.

"This is Penny," I mumbled when the classroom was finally quiet enough for Mr. Harrington to hear me. "Penny Hoffman. She's new."

"Pru and Penny," Mr. Harrington answered, as he kept thumping for quiet. "Pru and Penny," he repeated thoughtfully, abandoning the yardstick and stroking his beard as he gazed down at us with his pale blue eyes. I could hear, I thought, the trace of a British accent lingering in his voice from the years that—maybe—he had lived in England. Or had he?

"As alike," he continued, still examining us, "as two peas in a pod."

The class was about to snicker at this silly statement —but then suddenly Penny spoke up. As she did, she managed—brilliantly—to turn the class's attention on Mr. Harrington instead of on us.

"Oh," she said, stepping forward so energetically that the tassels from her sash bounced against her legs. "So you're Mr. Harrington! I've been wanting to meet you. You don't know how I've been looking forward to this. I've been wanting to meet you—ever since—ever since I read about you on the walls of the girls' bathroom!"

As a roar of hysterical laughter followed Penny's declaration, she and I managed to head down the aisle to two empty seats in the back of the room. I was glad to escape from all that staring, glad Penny had saved us. But still I was mystified. Just when in this over-eventful morning, I wondered, had she had time to see what was written on the walls of the girls' bathroom?

.2.

" 'Happy families are all alike,' " I was explaining
to Penny as she walked home from school with me that
day. "It's the beginning of a book, *Anna Karenina*—my
mom's favorite. Then the next part says, 'Every unhappy family is unhappy in its own way.' The book's
all sad and romantic. She—Anna—has this awful hus-
band and a handsome lover, and she finally commits
suicide by throwing herself under a train because she
can't find any way to make her family a happy one.

Some of the book is boring—not as good as *Green Mansions*. It's almost a thousand pages and has a whole chapter on jam-making, but . . . ."

"You sure talk a lot sometimes," Penny said, interrupting my monologue.

"I'm sorry," I answered.

Penny tossed her head in a lovely, jaunty way that made her hair swing forward and blow around her face. "Don't be," she told me pleasantly. "Just get to the point."

I nodded. "Mmm—yes, you're right. Well, the trouble with a happy family like mine is that there's never much excitement. Things can be bad at school, you see, but it never bothers me too much because at home they're always okay—okay but boring."

Penny didn't think it was going to be boring at our house. She couldn't wait, she'd been telling me all day, to get there and meet my family. All I was trying to do was prepare her a little for the nice, dull place to which I was taking her. Penny—even if she did look like me—was just so unusual and I didn't want her to be disappointed.

Because I could tell that she didn't want me rambling on about my family any more, we went back to laughing about how shocked Brooke had been to get into trouble for stealing Martha's books.

"Harrington can be a demon, can't he?" she asked me.

"Not often," I said, "but he sure was mad today."

"Because of Martha? Because it was Martha being teased?" As she asked these questions, she turned her green eyes on me.

I didn't answer. I couldn't. I was, all over again, amazed that this new friend of mine seemed to be able to look right into the middle of people's hearts and heads and see exactly what they were thinking or feeling. There was, as a matter of fact, some odd way in which Mr. Harrington pitied Martha and stood up for her. He also wrote poetry and stories for a magazine called *The Kenyon Review,* and someone (probably Cal Williams, when he wasn't peeing against a tree) had told me that Martha typed things for him to earn a little money. Maybe Harrington thought she needed the money because, instead of living with her parents, she lived with a crabby old aunt and grandmother. But Penny didn't know any of these things. We'd been much too busy having a super day at school—parading around, letting everyone examine the ways in which we looked alike—to talk about Martha.

"Not two peas—p-e-a-s—in a pod," Penny had kept explaining to the others. "Two *P*'s—just the letter *P* for Penny and *P* for Pru—in a pod."

In the schoolyard at lunch and recess we'd even, at

Penny's suggestion, walked in step next to one another, attracting so much attention that finally even Brooke and Alyson had to come to talk to us. It was right at that moment that the most astounding thing happened. Penny just turned her gleaming smile on Brooke and said, "I put Martha's books in your locker!"

Instead of being her usual terrible-tempered self when she heard this news, Brooke had simply laughed. Then the four of us ate lunch together—Brooke, Alyson, Penny, and me. It was one of my most impossible what-ifs—eating with A & B—and now that Penny was here, it had already happened.

"Look at that," Cal Williams had jeered as he slouched by. "The Ladybugs and the Peas all together. Do you know what happens when ladybugs run into peas? They crawl all over them, that's what. So watch out!"

I was feeling so good by then that I hardly even heard what Cal was saying because now for the first time in a year and a half I had a friend again. Not just an ordinary friend, but a special one who even looked like me. Brooke and Alyson didn't look anything alike, except that they each had freckles and wore identical enameled ladybugs in their pierced ears. To show everyone they were best friends, they always wore matching things. I'd been that way, too, back in Pittsburgh with Ruthie. We'd even had matching knotted wire rings we'd bought for one another.

My mom was going to go wild, I knew, to find me bringing a friend home. Especially someone like Penny. I always complained to Mom that I had no friends, and she always told me that all the people she knew who had pre-teen daughters told her that *their* daughters said the same thing. "Don't torture yourself, Prune, trying to get in good with kids like Alyson or Brooke who think they're so important. Find someone else. Someone with no special friend," she kept suggesting. "How about Martha Brandeberry, for instance?"

But I'd resisted. No friend at all was better, as far as I was concerned, than hooking up with a loser like Martha. And the wait had been worth it because finally the right kind of person had whirled into Mr. Harrington's homeroom and caught me up with her. How gloriously glorious things were going to be. That's what I was telling myself when the carton of oranges flipped out of the fruit and vegetable truck at Geneva right near my house.

Penny and I, minding our own business but yakking like a pair of parrots, had been swinging past old Sanguinetti's dented black pick-up when the oranges went thudding and rolling into the street. What a sight it was, with two dogs yapping and all the kids from the sidewalks running after the oranges. The kids weren't running to help the old man, either, but to steal the oranges. Poor Mr. Sanguinetti.

I wanted to stop and help, but Penny, taking my arm, shook her head. "Oh, not now, Pru—not today. Let somebody else help. I just can't wait to get to your house!"

Because we were almost home, I did as Penny said. "How did it happen, I wonder?" I said as I guided her into our front walk.

"What?"

"The oranges," I said, wondering how she could have forgotten about them so quickly.

"Don't know," she replied. "Probably some sneaky little kid who wanted one orange and accidentally tipped them all. Or who just wanted to do it. Haven't you ever wanted to do something like that—just to do it? Stand up in the middle of one of those stupid school symphonies and scream out loud? Break something just for the fun of beraking it? Or . . . ."

". . . write dirty words in wet cement?" I suggested, catching her enthusiasm as I took the key from the string around my neck and unlocked the front door. "Take your thumb and punch through the bottom of every chocolate in a box to see what's in it before you bite? In Pittsburgh, my friend Ruthie and I did that once."

As I was telling Penny about the chocolates, we breezed into the house to meet my family. (Well, my family except for my father, who was still downtown *in smog*. Frankly, some nights when he came home tired and a little cranky, my brother Lion and I felt he was still in smog. "Come home," we'd plead, "but leave the smog at the office.")

Mom was at the kitchen table painting an egg—a beautiful Chinese-y one—when she looked up and saw that there were two of me instead of just one. Egg-painting usually meant the fish writing wasn't going well, but since I wasn't alone, I knew she wouldn't be irritable. She wasn't.

"Holy Toledo," she cried, throwing down her fine-tipped brush and using one of the old-time expressions from her youth. "I'm seeing double! Everything but the faces!"

Linking arms, Penny and I laughed. Then I introduced her and watched, with my heart pounding, how happy I had just made my mother. I liked to make my mother happy.

I had been right in guessing she would love seeing me come in with a friend. "Not a cookie in the house," she mumbled apologetically, running her paint-flecked fingers through her short, curly black hair. "But I've got milk, and the cookies we can bake—right now. How about it? Find Lion. Li-on! Come here. Come see Prudie and her friend Penny. They're both in Ron Harrington's homeroom. Come see. You won't believe it. You won't believe how much they look alike!"

"Two P's in a pod," Penny explained, carefully spelling everything out. Then she left my side, bounced right up next to my mother, and asked what she could do to help with the cookies.

I didn't pinch Penny that afternoon—only myself, to make sure all these wonderful things were actually happening to me. I might have pinched Lion, though, for the way he behaved, except that I'd already bragged about my happy family and I didn't want him to tattle about my pinching and start a big argument.

Now, Lion—he's the family genius. He even goes to a special public school where he's part of what they call an "Impact Class." I do all right in school, and I read a lot, but since he's one of those super IQ kids, he decided he'd better show Penny that right away. First he walked around her in circles staring at her wide-eyed, with his mouth hanging open.

Then he said, "So what's the big deal? They both have black hair. Penny here—she's at least a centimeter shorter, half a stone heavier—and her nose is bigger."

If Penny was upset at his comments, she didn't say so; she just laughed and looked down her slightly-longer nose at my chubby, sandy-haired nine-year-old brother. Then she did something he hated. She reached out and rumpled up his already wild mane of hair. Lion hated having anyone touch his head—even Mom or Dad—and somehow Penny, as she knew things about other people, knew that, too.

"If you're a lion," she told him, taking her hand off his head and going back to her job of adding flour to the cookie batter, "that wasn't much of a roar. Let me hear you roar."

Mom chuckled and looked over at Penny with a crinkly-eyed smile. She was in some kind of parent-paradise, her head filled with visions of laughing children, cold milk, and hot cookies spreading out over an endless series of afternoons. You see, Mom—like me—was always quick to see the what-if possibilities of any situation. She was so pleased, this particular afternoon, that she didn't even flinch when Penny dropped the subject of lions and mentioned that she and I were thinking of having our ears pierced. (We were?) Oh, I wanted to, but I was terribly afraid of needles and pain. Besides, Daddy had—time and time again—absolutely forbidden me to have it done. When the subject of ear-piercing failed to alarm Mom, I found myself watching her and Penny and the obviously disgruntled Lion.

As I watched, I felt an odd tingle running into my toes and the tips of my fingers. "What if . . . ," I began to ask myself, "what if . . . things don't work out and . . . ?"

My fearful what-if was never quite finished because Penny, swinging her hair behind her shoulders, suddenly went back to a discussion of lions and the noises they make. "Come on, come on," she urged my brother. "Let me hear you roar."

Backing away from her, blinking his eyes rapidly and rubbing at his rounded stomach, he answered. His voice, however, came out in a tight little whisper. "I don't roar. I never roar. Not all lions roar. Sometimes they just scratch. I scratch." To illustrate his words, he held up his fingers in a threatening, clawlike manner. "But if I scratch you," he told Penny, "I may not like what I find!"

We tried to laugh and make excuses for Lion's rudeness. Poor Lion—he didn't have much in the way of a friend, either, except for me, so now he was terribly, terribly jealous. Excuses or no excuses, however, my brother's words spread some of my dad's leftover smog over the rest of the afternoon.

First, two trays of cookies burned because someone had accidentally shoved the oven temperature dial from three hundred fifty to four seventy-five. Then, just when the blackened cookies had been emptied into the garbage, something else—something much more serious —happened.

The egg toppled off the kitchen table and smashed into a hundred million little pieces. It wasn't just any egg, you see, but the very special eight-color one my mom had been working on for almost two weeks. It had a design with peacocks taken from an old Chinese plate and was, as my dad kept saying, a true work of art. But now it was nothing. Nothing but scraps of multicolored confetti crunching under our feet.

" 'Not all the king's horses, Nor all the king's men . . . ,' " Mom was mumbling to herself as—with a blob of dried scarlet-colored paint between her eyes— she kept winking to hold back the tears.

"But how did it happen?" I asked myself. Even though *I'd* been nowhere near the table but at the sink washing batter from the mixing bowls, I found myself rushing over, bending down, and trying to scoop up the now worthless fragments.

"Oh, I'm so sorry," I said, beginning to babble aloud. "Oh, Mom, Mom. . . . I'm so sorry about your egg. . . ."

Why I was the one down on the floor apologizing, I can't tell you. Worried that maybe poor, jealous Lion had smashed it because he hated Penny. Worried that Penny, my new but still unknown friend, had done it accidentally.

As I was gathering up the fragments, still saying "I'm sorry," I suddenly realized that Penny was hugging my upset, moist-eyed mother. Hugging her lovingly as I often did. I couldn't see the face, only the thin body and the heavy black hair. It was so odd, so unexplainably odd to be kneeling on the floor, looking up at myself hugging my mother. Lion saw it, too. Suddenly, as if he was very cold, he began to squeeze his arms across his chest.

As Penny was clutching at my mother, she was weeping. Weeping and talking in a choked-up voice. "Oh, Mrs. Phillips, Mrs. Phillips. I did it. I did it. My elbow —my stupid, clumsy elbow. How can you forgive me? How can you ever forgive me?"

Penny continued to plead tearfully, but I could see she had already been forgiven. My mother was rocking her gently, pushing damp hair away from the side of her face. In our house, you see, honest mistakes owned-up-to were always generously forgiven.

But something about the scene spooked Lion so much he turned and fled to his room. I almost felt like doing the same, yet I didn't. I continued to crunch the bits of eggshell between my fingers. "What if . . . Lion did it to get Penny into trouble? What if . . . Penny is covering up for Lion—but why would she? What if . . . she . . . ?"

"Here, Pru, don't you do it. I must," Penny cried, wiping her tears as she pulled away from my mother. "It was *me*—all stupid, all clumsy—and the least I can do, the very least, is pick up. Give that stuff to me— here!"

As she was speaking, she dropped down to where I was kneeling. Then with quick, careful fingers she began collecting the remaining scattered fragments. "Some beginning I've made," she fretted, staring at me with her now swollen red-and-green eyes.

I looked up and saw Mom, the tragedy of her shattered masterpiece softened by the vision of two dark-haired girls kneeling together on her kitchen floor. She smiled down at us through her tears.

Her smile made the warm feeling begin to flow back inside my chest as Penny and I shared the burden of a precious egg my brother had no doubt smashed. Gently, I bumped my shoulder against Penny's. "No," I told her softly. "Accidents happen. Forget it. I think you've made a wonderful beginning."

"I LOVE YOUR HOUSE, PRU. YOUR HOUSE AND YOUR FAMILY. Especially your family." Over and over Penny kept telling me that during the first month we were in school together.

She made sure that my family loved her, too. Starting with Mom. Somehow Penny had managed to save all the pitiful chips from the broken Chinese egg. Then, as a surprise, she glued and lacquered them onto a little copper disc, which she gave to my mother to wear around her neck on a grosgrain ribbon.

After that, she'd made peace with Lion by bringing him a jigsaw puzzle, which was a real challenge. She'd made it out of a sheet of shirt cardboard. The thing that was so challenging was that the puzzle had no picture at all. It was nothing but the natural speckled cardboard cut into teeny-tiny shapes. Some of the shapes were regulation-type jigsaw pieces with the little in-squiggles and out-squiggles, but some of them were cut to look like spaceships or camels or monster faces. It must have taken her hours—just hours—to make it for him.

Even my father found Penny quite acceptable. Particularly after he overheard her telling me he was even handsomer than Mr. Harrington. He only frowned at us when she or I brought up the subject of ear-piercing.

"A savage, mutilating custom," he kept insisting. "If you're determined to pierce something, girls, you might as well pierce your noses and wear gaudy golden rings hanging down from them!"

Whenever he made this joke, Penny never argued. Instead, she always laughed as if it was the very first time she had heard it. (My dad just loves when people laugh at his terrible jokes.) Privately, when Penny wasn't around, Dad would give me one of his slightly overenthusiastic squeezes and tell me that although Penny and I looked alike, I was still prettier. "I like your little button nose," he'd tell me. That was his unsubtle way of being subtle and not saying, as Lion had, that Penny's nose was longer. I was getting tired of that comment, however, because people who compared us at school always made nose jokes, too.

Since Penny loved my house so much, she kept coming home from school with me and putting off having me come to her apartment. Though I was terribly eager to see her place and meet her parents, I didn't argue, but I did keep *reminding* her.

"Soon," she always told me. "When we get more settled—we did just move, you know—and when my father's feeling better. Maybe after the field trip to the elephant seals. How about it, huh?"

Penny wasn't making excuses. It wasn't as if she was ashamed of her apartment or her parents. Her life was just a little more complicated than mine. Because her father had this awful breathing problem, he couldn't work or climb steps, so he was home all the time while her mother worked as an accountant for a trucking company. There were older sisters, too, but they both lived away from home. One worked and one was in college studying veterinary medicine.

Of course, we didn't talk families all of the time while we were getting to know each other. Not even most of the time. We didn't talk books, either, the way

Ruthie and I used to do—because Penny read only science fiction, and I read only romantic novels. Mostly we talked about movies, which we both loved, and about Brooke, Alyson, Martha, and Mr. Harrington. Especially Mr. Harrington. Penny said she didn't like him but that he interested her. At my house, sometimes she'd ask Mom about him and their Tuesday night writers' group. At school, she always paid strict attention in his class and laughed at his bad jokes. It was all part of what Penny called *strategy,* and it was *very important.*

Penny, Penny—I know I keep saying Penny, but that's all I could think of most of the time. The first moment I saw her she had told me she was a leader, and it was true. Some people, like her, seem to be natural leaders and some, like me, always seem to be followers. But I didn't mind. I swear. How could anyone mind following someone as fascinating as Penny Hoffman? She was so full of energy and surprising ideas. She had lots of strategies, too—all unique.

"Dressing alike is nerdy," she told me very soon after we became friends, "especially since we are alike anyway. But—*trading* is chic."

After she explained to me that *chic* meant "fashionable and classy," we began to trade. Some days I wore her coiling scarf around my head or waist and she wore the bright patchwork sweater Mom had knitted for me. Other days I'd wear her slightly-too-tight blue clogs and she'd wear my too-wide striped tennis shoes. Or I'd wear her necklace of sea-urchin spines while she wore my macramé collar. It was a good strategy. It confused people.

From a distance, particularly if we weren't together, sometimes people didn't know which one of us was which. Mr. Harrington seemed to find this funny. Sometimes when we came into homeroom, he'd say something. Sometimes he'd just wink. This chic trading interested Brooke and Alyson, too, but not quite in the same way that it did Harrington.

Despite our one lunch together, they had never become friends with Penny or me. They'd say "hi" if we passed them, but mostly they whispered a lot and seemed jealous of all the attention *we* were getting. The Ladybugs tried so hard to be alike by dressing in matching clothes, but it was rather silly looking because Brooke was stringbean skinny with straight brown hair, while Alyson was short and potato-shaped with stiff red hair.

Penny's strategy for dealing with them involved what she called "being nice but never pushy." *We* talked to everyone—even to Martha Brandeberry. Martha's dark eyes always looked a little glassy when we talked to her. She never seemed very grateful as I would have been if I'd been a nerd like Martha and had a superstar like Penny paying attention to me. Instead, she looked quietly suspicious.

That was exactly how she was looking the day of the field trip to the elephant seals. It was a day for a *new strategy*, Penny had told me before school when we, as usual, sat talking on the fender of Mr. Harrington's two-tone Chevy. The first part was asking Martha to sit with us on the bus. After Penny got very enthusiastic and persuasive, Martha finally agreed. Doing it, however, wasn't as easy as asking because those seats were made for two, not three. Even though Penny and I were thin, it was a tight squeeze to include Martha, who had a wide bottom to match her wide, fully developed chest. Yet, as we twisted along down Highway #1, there she sat next to us in her green skirt, leotard, and scuffed-toe ballet shoes.

We were sitting right in the middle of the bus because we'd turned up our noses at the idea of struggling—like Brooke, Alyson, or Cal Williams and some of the bigger boys—to grab for the back seats. In the front, not too far ahead of us, sat Mr. Harrington and our principal, Mrs. Noreen Monzoni (somewhere there was a Mr. Monzoni, but we'd never seen him). Mrs. Monzoni was along to replace Mrs. Kremenski, the other sixth-grade homeroom teacher. Kremenski was staying behind because she said the trip would be hard on her varicose veins. So, together Harrington and Mrs. M. were going to escort us down the coast past Pescadero to Ano Nuevo State Park, where we could see a beach and an island full of 400-pound elephant seals. It was to be, Harrington had been telling us for a month, a very special treat.

Penny said she wasn't going to be interested in ugly elephant seals whose noses were so long they dragged in their mouths, so I knew I wouldn't like them, either. What Penny was interested in was Mr. Harrington. That's why Martha had been invited to sit with us.

I had already, weeks ago, told Penny everything I knew about him. Ronald B. Harrington—six feet tall (about), one hundred and sixty pounds (about), forty (maybe) years old. A bachelor with a slight British accent and a two-tone green Chevy, but no television set and no telephone. He didn't believe in them. He didn't believe in driving to school, either, but he didn't have to because he lived in a third-story flat—on the top floor—right across from the schoolyard, which was why his car was always parked right where it was. "Maybe it doesn't even run," I told Penny. "I've never seen him drive it."

"Not even on dates?" Penny had asked, implying in

her strange-smart way that she knew the answer.

"He doesn't date—as far as I know, at least."

"Not even pretty foxes like Mrs. Monzoni?"

"No," I had answered, because all I knew about Ronald B. Harrington ended just about there—except for the rumors. And there were lots of them around Portola Hill. Rumors about a wife and a daughter lost in some kind of terrible accident. Or a sick wife locked up in a mental institution. There were even a few rumors about him not liking women because maybe he only liked men. It was just as impossible for the other students as it was for me to see a tall, handsome, bearded teacher who lived all alone and wrote for *The Kenyon Review* without doing a great deal of what-iffing about him.

Whenever I asked Mom about the Harrington rumors, she'd just laugh and say, "Why I don't have the faintest idea, Prudie. Where do you get these wild ideas? Out of those books you've been reading?"

Despite the rumors, though, and the way my mother dismissed them, Harrington was very popular. Some of the girls even had a thing about him. But, still, he was big stuff with the boys, too, because he liked to play basketball with them in the yard after school. In some weird way, he seemed to like everybody and nobody, if that's possible. He was, in short, as I have been saying at great length—a True Man of Mystery.

That's why Martha had been selected. Today's strategy was to *pump Martha for information*—any kind of information about Harrington. Over the rickety rumbling of the bus and the yelling of our classmates, it was quite easy for Penny to start her quizzing.

"You do some typing for him sometimes, don't you?" Penny asked, pointing toward the front seat where he sat talking with pretty little Mrs. Monzoni. Her name sounded like some kind of Italian pasta, but she usually looked more like a piece of French pastry. Today, to see the elephant seals, she was wearing her pale lavender pantsuit with a ruffly white blouse.

"Equal opportunity for women" was Penny's explanation of how such a sweet, yellow-haired twenty-eight (about)-year-old pastry had already become an elementary school principal.

Martha's answer to Penny's question about the typing was very brief. "Sometimes," she admitted, looking as if her teeth were half stuck together with gummy candy.

"What kinds of things?" Penny asked after a long pause during which she gazed out the window toward the ocean, pretending that what Martha typed for Harrington wasn't very important. I knew she was playing cat-and-mouse with Martha because of the soft jabs she kept giving me with her right elbow.

Without being too obvious, I tried to peek past Penny and get a look at Martha's face. She might be a mouse—a nerdy mouse—but she wasn't dumb, and to me she didn't look at all taken in by Penny's approach.

"What kinds of things what?" Martha answered, rubbing the worn toes of her ballet shoes against one another.

"Do you type for him?" Penny said, all cheerful and smiling as if she weren't the least bit annoyed by Martha's unwillingness to talk about Harrington.

Martha was silent for a minute. Then she shrugged. "Just things. I don't pay much attention."

"Well, what about his flat?" Penny asked, beginning to press just a little harder. "Have you seen it? Been there? What's it like? Full of books? Of *Playboy* magazines? Or . . . or other kinds—with other kinds of pictures?"

I could see a little twitch next to Martha's right eye, but she didn't answer Penny's questions. Instead, she pulled the rounded neck of her black leotard up a little higher. Then, twisting her hands together and letting them drop in her lap, she simply closed her eyes.

Watching Penny's disappointed face and Martha's reaction to her questioning about Mr. Harrington made me feel all excited. Without stopping to think that I might be messing up Penny's strategy, I suddenly began talking. "Have you, Martha? Have you ever seen the inside of Harrington's flat? Was he alone? Was he with Mrs. Monzoni? Do they see each other secretly? I read about things like that in books sometimes. Do you think maybe there's something going on between them? What if . . . he and she are . . . ?"

"Shut up," Penny said, nudging me gently.

"I'm sorry," I said, smiling at her, knowing I'd been a bit carried away and knowing that only Penny could say "shut up" in such a soft, non-insulting way.

When I finished apologizing to Penny, I saw that Martha's eyes were open again. She was staring straight ahead, up toward the front of the wildly noisy sixth-grade-filled bus where Ronald Harrington and Noreen Monzoni (looking, I thought, a little like Vronsky and Anna Karenina), oblivious to the din, were deeply involved in some serious discussion.

"Oh, Pru," Penny urged, using her nicest, friendliest voice. "Don't upset Martha. Don't ask her about *them*. Can't you see that it upsets Martha to see them together? It makes her worry about poor Mr. Monzoni. Doesn't it, Martha?"

Martha didn't answer. She just sat there, but her face turned custard yellow, as if she were about to become disgustingly sick from the lurching of the bus.

Then Penny, suddenly totally relaxed and casual, slumped forward and began unwinding her gauzy headdress. "Want to wear it for a while?" she asked me. "It's giving me a headache today. Trade you for your blue barrettes, huh?"

Something had just happened. Penny's strategy was over. She had managed to find out exactly what she wanted to know from Martha the Nerd, who'd hardly said anything. Right then I felt as nerdy as Martha for not being as smart and subtle as Penny.

"What if . . . ?" I began asking myself as the bus sped on, bringing us closer to a meeting with a herd of ugly elephant seals, "for once *I* could come up with strategies? What if . . . ?"

"Pru, Pru," Penny said, shaking me slightly. "Are you there? I just asked you whether Saturday would be a good day for having our ears pierced."

"Hmmm," I answered, wondering how she could already be talking about the ear-piercing I'd been forbidden to have done while I was still staring stupidly at Mr. Harrington and Mrs. Monzoni.

AFTER WE'D ALL PUSHED AND SHOVED OUR WAY OUT OF the bus at Ano Nuevo and been introduced to Ms. Lainie Torres, the U.S. Ranger who was to be our guide, Mr. Harrington said we had to pair up two by two because the path to the elephant seal beach wasn't very wide.

"We wouldn't want to do any ecological damage," he told us, standing right next to Mrs. Monzoni but smiling over toward Ms. Torres.

Harrington's announcement didn't bother me at all

because for the first time since I'd come to San Francisco, I didn't have to worry about who my partner would be. Penny was at my side smiling at me. We just stood there together watching as our classmates milled around whistling and hand-flapping until everyone had a partner. Everyone except (of course) Martha Brandeberry. Almost before this became obvious, Penny took hold of the sleeve of my parka and marched us right up to Harrington.

"Let Martha walk with us," she pleaded. "She shouldn't be left alone. You and Mrs. Monzoni and Ms. Torres are *three*. If the three of you and the three of us sort of walk together that would make six—three pairs, and no one's feelings would be hurt." Penny's voice was distinct but still soft enough that Martha couldn't hear.

Without even pausing to rub at his beard, Mr. Harrington agreed. He didn't say anything. He just nodded at Penny with a strange, slightly puzzled look. He was, I decided then and there, probably surprised but appreciative that his newest student was sensitive enough to show consideration for the class nerd.

Because of Harrington's nod, Penny and I ended up walking right near the front—just where we (according to Penny) wanted to be. When the six of us paired off, the result was pretty funny, actually. Ms. Torres asked Mr. Harrington and Mrs. Monzoni to go first. Then, maybe thinking Penny and I were non-identical twins or something, she didn't split us up. She walked with Martha at her side and we, the two P's, followed them. Behind us came the other thirty-eight, plus two more rangers whose names I never heard.

Some of us, including Mrs. Monzoni, had been under the impression that we were going to step out of the bus, walk about seventy-two feet, and say, "Hey, look at the elephant seals!" But we were wrong. The walk out to see them turned out to be three-fourths of a mile each way over a muddy path full of stones and chuck-holes. When the path disappeared, we had to start slogging our way up and down over endless, humpy, wet sand dunes.

Poor Mrs. Monzoni in that lavender outfit and a pair of strappy sandals with two-inch heels. Almost before we started, her feet were mucky and her pants polka-dotted with splotches of mud. Mr. Harrington had to keep grabbing for her elbow to help her as she picked her unsteady way along the trail. When we hit the dunes, she had even more problems. They were slippery, and Harrington had to hold on to her practically the whole time to keep her from sinking in up to her knees or just rolling off into the ocean.

Martha's thin little ballet slippers with their bands

of elastic sewn across the top were not much better, I noticed, than Mrs. Monzoni's sandals. Martha, too, had a terrible struggle through the mud and across the sand. But, since Ms. Torres didn't reach out to help her as Harrington was helping Mrs. M., she had to manage alone.

Ms. Torres was so busy explaining to Martha all about the breeding cycles of elephant seals and about the sixty-five-pound newborn pups (born right on the island and beach at Ano Nuevo) who nurse for twenty-nine days on milk that is fifty-five percent fat, that she never noticed Martha was having trouble. She just kept on talking. I even overheard her saying that the pups gain almost three hundred pounds in those twenty-nine days, but that sounded like a big *fat* lie to me, I decided, as I was copying Penny by watching Martha watching Harrington and Mrs. Monzoni.

The intelligently boring Ms. Torres kept chattering on, but Martha didn't even nod or turn to look at her. She just stared straight ahead as she stumbled and slipped along. She should have been cold with no sweater or parka to cover up her leotard, but she hadn't brought one. All she had was a shabby old purse that hung from her left shoulder. Poor Martha. At times like this I always found myself feeling sorry for her because she had to live with a dried-up aunt and grandmother instead of the kind of nice, thoughtful parents who would never let a daughter leave for a field trip to the beach without a warm sweater or jacket. (It wasn't that Martha didn't have parents—she did. But they were separated. Her father, who worked for the Post Office, lived alone, and her mother lived down near Golden Gate Fields, where she worked grooming horses.)

Martha, Martha—I didn't want to waste my day worrying about her, I began reminding myself; but there she was, totally unprotected from the cold February wind and tongues of damp, low-lying fog that were licking the tops of the dunes. And all the way out she never shivered even once. As I kept my eyes on the back of her leotard waiting for a shiver—even a little one—I did begin to see that Penny's reasons for quizzing Martha had been to understand *for sure* whether there was any lovey-dovey stuff going on between Harrington and our foxy, yellow-headed principal. As soon as I had that at least partially cleared up inside my head, I was tempted to turn to Penny and go on to another subject. I wanted to ask just how she thought I was going to get my ears pierced on Saturday without my parents' permission.

But I didn't ask. I had to continue trying to keep up with Penny and her fast-clicking brain. As we walked, she winked and smiled at me whenever I looked over at her. She also made her hair swing in that wonderful way of hers. A couple of times, I smiled back and tried to shake my hair exactly as she did. I couldn't quite do it. Nor—I discovered as we got farther and farther out onto the dunes where the wind was fiercer—could I keep my nose from running, and I had no Kleenex. My nose wouldn't stop dripping as the damp, cold wind blew into my face, but Penny's didn't seem to be affected at all.

Penny saved me, though, from having to use the sleeve of my parka in the embarrassing way Lion would have done. As she always knew everything, she knew, even before my nose leaked visibly onto my upper lip, that I was in trouble.

"Martha," she called up ahead. "Got a tissue?"

Yes, of course Martha had a tissue. In her shoulder bag. As she took it out and turned back to hand it to Penny, her face looked less blank than usual. In fact, it looked very distressed.

Penny took the Kleenex and handed it to me, but she kept on looking at Martha. "I'm sorry it bothers you to see *them*," she said softly. "Would you like Pru and me to walk in front of you?"

"No," Martha said, turning away with a strange, jerking motion, as if—in all this cold—she'd been burned by leaning against a too hot stove. Then, as if she was suddenly aware that Penny and I were watching her, she turned her head and began to nod with interest as Ms. Torres told her that from 1884 until the 1930's elephant seals bred only on the island of Guadalupe, off the coast of Baja California.

As I was wiping my nose with Martha's Kleenex, Penny turned and gave me one of her special smiles. "You do understand, don't you, Pru?" she asked.

"Of course," I answered happily as we approached the last high dune before the elephant seal beach.

By the time we had conquered the final dune, Ms. Torres had started explaining to the whole group that this was as far as we were allowed to go. "The tide is exceptionally high and dangerous today," she told us. "Besides, we've been having trouble with students reaching out and touching the animals, and that can be extremely dangerous, too. The bulls have violent tempers."

Staying up on top of the dune was quite all right with me, I decided, the very instant I looked down. The elephant seals on the beach below us and on the offshore island were huge! Huge and with wrinkly gray skin and those horribly hideous, enormous, droopy snouts.

"What a problem *they* must have with runny noses," I whispered to Penny.

"Ssh!" she said with a little frown. "We should listen so Harrington won't have a fit."

Personally, I would have rather risked Harrington's temper and made a few jokes because I found the elephant seals just as awful as Penny had predicted. There seemed to be hundreds of them all over the beach and island. Most of them were just lying there like old gray rocks, but some were creeping, wriggling, and rolling about. A lot of the females were nursing these huge, blimpy babies from fat, saggy breasts. On the island some of the bulls were fighting, chewing ferociously into one another with long, pointed fangs. The bulls on the beach below us were all cut up and bloody-looking.

"It's called Losers' Beach," Ms. Torres told us, "because the bulls who lose out in their fight for a female to mate with come here to lick their wounds."

As she talked and I saw those bloody bulls, looking as if they weighed a thousand pounds, instead of just four hundred, I was glad all over again that we were way up on a dune and the tide was too high to go any closer. To give us that closer look, though, Ms. Torres and the other rangers were offering us field glasses.

When my turn came, I passed them on without looking. I didn't need glasses to examine them any closer.

Nor did I need them to see that, despite their size and ugliness, elephant seals seemed to be very sexy beasts. Several of the enormous males and females were mating on the island right in front of us. They'd raise their heads, make terrible noises, and then just go at it. As you can imagine, the boys—especially Cal Williams and his crew—were hooting and howling at the mating and the fat female breasts as poor Ms. Torres struggled to give us her well-prepared lecture.

Of course, I'd heard most of it already on the way out as she'd tried it out on Martha, so I didn't listen. All I could think of as I swabbed my nose with the Kleenex that was getting limper and limper was how dizzy I was beginning to feel trapped up on that high dune looking down at the ugly creatures below. I hate heights. They give me the creeps.

I turned and whispered to Penny, "I hate heights."

"Later," she whispered back softly.

Then, before I could ask what she meant, she had moved away from my side and over toward Mr. Harrington and Mrs. Monzoni. "This is wonderful," she told them breathlessly, with her eyes sparkling. "It's all so *natural* and exciting. I mean—well, you know—it shows that sex and everything is beautiful and just part of life!"

Mrs. Monzoni reddened and looked distinctly uncomfortable as Penny enthused. I couldn't believe what I was hearing, either, because Penny had sworn she was going to hate this field trip, yet she sounded so sincere. Yes, she *was* sincere. She was loving every minute of it, even if I wasn't. I was sure we didn't look alike then. My eyes weren't shining. My cheeks hadn't turned pink from the wind—only my nose.

Watching Penny's energy affect Harrington and Mrs. M., looking at the elephant seals, and feeling dizzy had almost made me forget about Martha when suddenly, Brooke's distinctive, boyishly gruff voice rose above the sound of the wind and the other voices. "Martha looks like a sea elephant," she said.

It had been predictable, entirely predictable, that someone would say that. I had thought of it myself. In fact, I'd been about to whisper it to Penny when I was interrupted by more leaking from my nose. Now, though, we were going to have a scene because Brooke had said it *out loud*. Harrington was going to explode. Absolutely explode.

But before he could rub at his beard and say a word, Penny spoke. Her voice was different than I'd ever heard it before. It was tough and savage.

"Who said that?" she demanded, knowing full well. "Was it you, Brooke? Was it? You? How would you like it if someone made fun of you? How would you like it, huh? You know what, Brooke Cole—you're just jealous, jealous of Martha and her beautiful figure!"

I didn't have to raise my eyes to see the approving looks I knew must be flooding over the faces of Harrington and Mrs. Monzoni. Nor did I have to look at Penny, who had not been the least bit afraid to stand up to Brooke and who, like a true leader, understood that even nerds have rights.

"I have so much to learn from Penny," I told myself gratefully as Ms. Torres tried to resume her lecture. "I am so lucky."

As I was pinching myself to make myself believe my good luck, I let my eyes slide over to where Martha was standing slightly to one side by herself. She looked as if she were in another world and had not heard a single word. I realized for the first time that Penny, as always, had been right. Martha did have a figure *some* people might be jealous of. Her waist was small. It was just her hips and chest that were so large, and . . . well . . . most sixth-grade girls—including Brooke, Alyson, Penny, and me—simply didn't look that way.

For a very long minute I stared at her. Standing alone with the wind whipping her hair about her face and the fog swirling behind her full green skirt, she might have stepped out of *Jane Eyre*. Using only the slightest what-if, I could see her on a misty English moor instead of a California sand dune.

"Martha . . . ," I said, moving several steps closer to her and feeling my hair and the tassels from Penny's scarf swinging in almost the proper way. I didn't know what I was going to say to her—just something nice. Something Penny and Mr. Harrington would approve of.

But Martha didn't even blink at the sound of my voice. She was staring, as if hypnotized, down at the masses of ugly elephant seals. Down toward a spot where one slightly isolated female was nursing a pup so young it had no snout. In fact, it had a sweet little face—an adorable face and soft, velvety skin. When I looked back up, Martha was still looking down at it. Her face was weirdly dreamy-looking between its strands of windblown brownish-blond hair.

"Martha . . . ," I repeated, but as I said her name again, I could feel Penny moving up next to me.

Then her fingers touched my elbow. "Don't get carried away," she warned me softly. "Strategy, strategy."

I didn't have the teeniest idea what she meant. The minute I got a few things straight, Penny always seemed to mix me up again. Puzzled, I turned away from Martha, looked at Harrington and Mrs. Monzoni, who were still standing close together, and then, finally, looked back into the green eyes of my look-alike. "I'm sorry," I said.

"Why do you always say that?" Penny asked.

"What?"

" 'I'm sorry.' "

Trying to decide whether I was annoying her, I wiped at my nose. She didn't look annoyed. Not in the least. "I don't know," I admitted. "I won't if you don't like it. I'm sorry."

As I was apologizing for apologizing, Penny started to laugh, just a soft, comfortable chuckle, so I laughed, too. I didn't have the faintest idea why we were laughing. But if something was funny enough to make her—Penny—laugh, then I—Pru—would mirror her by laughing along with her.

.5.

IT WAS, FOR ME, A VERY UNUSUAL WEEK. MONDAY MORN-
ing I went to see elephant seals and Tuesday—before
8:15—I went to the men's bathroom with Mr. Harrington. I had been sitting on the fender of his Chevy Tuesday waiting for Penny, eager to talk with her about the
thing going on between him and Mrs. Monzoni, and
then before I knew it, he and I were alone in the room
with the door marked *Teachers' Room: Men*.

It was strange, all right, but not quite as weird as it
sounds. I can explain everything. You see, he had come

up behind me, and in a tight-lipped way had said that he needed to talk with me privately. He had never talked to me privately before, except at his desk a couple of times after class. Those times, he'd asked me to stay behind and then quietly told me how impressed he'd been with one of my what-if stories. (Oh, yes, that was what I did best at school—wrote these crazy pretend stories, usually being brave enough or stupid enough to use the names or nicknames of the classmates I was what-iffing about.)

"Very impressive," he'd said to me each of those private times as he'd rubbed thoughtfully at his beard. "Naïve but impressive."

Now, however, he looked very upset as he told me that this chat of ours had to be "totally private." Totally private couldn't be anywhere but the bathroom for men teachers. Because Harrington was the only male teacher at Portola Hill, it meant no one could possibly interrupt us if we talked there. Also, since the room marked *Teachers' Room: Men* was actually two rooms, we didn't have to stand and lean against the the sink and toilet as we talked. The other, non-toilet, part had a couch, a chair, a table, and a coffee pot.

But, still, we didn't begin our private talk in the part with the couch. We had to go and stand right next to the toilet because someone had taken a wide-tipped red felt pen and written something on the wall just behind it.

"Ronald H. loves Noreen M.," said the bold letters on the wall.

"Pru?" Harrington asked as we backed out of the toilet room and moved toward the couch. "Who could have done something like that? Who? Mrs. Monzoni tells me that the same thing is in the women teachers' lounge and in all the student bathrooms. It's a slanderous lie. And very embarrassing, too. Very. Would you like a cup of coffee?"

"No, I don't drink," I answered, attempting to make a feeble joke while I tried to figure out whether he was accusing me.

As he looked over at me, he was rubbing at his beard and looking terribly handsome in a nubby brown tweed suit with a yellow shirt and speckly brown tie. Most of the time his handsomeness didn't get to me, but whenever he got that troubled, thoughtful look, which made him seem to be a real suffering poet, then it did.

"I only asked you, Pru," he began to explain, "because you seem to understand things about people that some of the other students don't. . . ."

"Me?" I answered in a rusty-sounding voice. *I* didn't understand things about people. Penny did. "He couldn't have confused us, could he?" I asked myself.

"Confused us because I'm still wearing Penny's scarf?"

"Pru!" he said. "Are you listening to me? This is dreadfully important. Listen—Mrs. Monzoni is a married woman, and gossip like this isn't funny. It's lethal. Deadly. This is no game. Someone very cruel has done this thing. I'm appealing to you, Pru, because I feel you are honest. Now . . . who would have defaced these walls with red ink? Who?"

No, he didn't have me mixed up with Penny. It was a very interesting situation, actually. I would have liked to put down my book bag, lean back, and soak up the whole scene. But he was not going to give me the time to do so.

"Who? Who?" he repeated urgently.

"I don't know," I said. I did know, of course, or thought I did. I knew who always used red pens—the Ladybugs, Brooke and Alyson. They used red pens for everything, since red was the color of ladybugs.

"Dull," Penny always said about the red ink business. "Childish and unoriginal."

Not everyone in our class felt that way, though. Lots of the other girls had thought it was smart and copied A & B by turning in their papers in red ink, too. So the Ladybugs didn't *have* to be the villains who had written on the bathroom walls. But probably they were. (Why, I had even bought a red pen and tried it on one of my papers, but that was before Penny came. Now I used brown ink, while she used purple because she said brown and purple were classy colors.)

Thinking of Penny made me suddenly wonder just what she would say if she were the one sitting in the men's room with Harrington. Then I shivered as I found myself about to ask—as Penny might have—"Well, *is* there anything going on between you and Mrs. Monzoni?"

I didn't say it, though. I just bit down on my tongue and shook my head violently. Then, jumping to my feet, I started toward the door. "No," I insisted. "I don't know. I don't know."

I had to get out of there quickly before I gave in to the temptation to tattle. I had reason enough to do so, too, because it was Alyson's twelfth birthday today. To celebrate, she and Brooke had invited all the girls in the class to a lunchtime yard party. All except for Martha, Penny, and me. I knew it was more than possible that the potato-shaped redhead had started the day off by writing on the bathroom walls. Besides, I would have loved to accuse her—guilty or not. But although I was sometimes a little nerdy, I had never been, nor did I intend to be, a fink.

Somehow, as I was thinking these things, Mr. Harrington had managed to get to the door before I did.

He stood there blocking my way and looking down at me with those terribly serious blue eyes. Blue eyes set deeply into his thin face—a face surrounded by wavy, graying hair and a beard.

"Pru . . . ," he said, looking somehow weirdly helpless. "Pru . . . your friend Penny . . . . Listen, I wish I . . . ."

He wanted to tell me something. I could see that, and what he was suffering, trying not to tell me, was not simply about red ink on a wall behind a toilet.

"What if . . . he is desperate to confide in someone about his passion for Mrs. Monzoni, but he's afraid I'll tell Penny?" I asked myself. "What if . . . he's thinking of taking his Chevy and running off with Mrs. M. and needs my help?"

He was almost shaking as he stood there in front of me with his eyes beginning to look sort of watery. Not only was Ronald B. Harrington a True Man of Mystery, but at this very moment he was a Desperate, Unhappy True Man of Mystery.

Just then another horrible but exciting idea started whirling around inside my head. "What if . . . it's *me*? What if . . . he has some kind of thing for *me*—because of my stories (naïve and impressive) and my insight?"

I stood there half expecting him to declare his insane, passionate love for me and ask me to run away with him in his '58 two-tone. He was so handsomely troubled—so Mr. Rochester-looking—that I almost would have pretended I was Jane Eyre and gone off with him, too. Except . . . except . . . .

". . . I would have had to explain that my parents wouldn't let me," I was telling Penny at lunch, which was the first moment we'd had alone all day. "Because if they won't even let me pierce my ears—they certainly wouldn't have let me run off and live in sin with *him!*"

Penny and I were laughing (and laughing in the noisiest way) as I told her all about my private, early-morning bathroom talk with Harrington. I hadn't been able to tell her before because by the time I'd squeezed past him and escaped, the second bell had already rung. Now was a good time, anyway, to be telling her and laughing because now Alyson's birthday party was going on in the sunny south corner of the yard.

They were all clumped together over there—A & B and the rest of the sixth-grade girls—where they had paper napkins with strawberries on them. (They had strawberries because no one had been able to find napkins decorated with ladybugs!) They also had red strawberry soda along with red-hot cinnamon candies and tiny black jelly beans. To annoy the girls, Cal Williams and some of the boys kept hanging around begging for candy and sips of soda.

"He was incredible—absolutely incredible!" I told Penny, following my statement with another loud laugh.

"Ssh! Keep your voice down," Penny told me as she began to unbutton my patchwork sweater, which she was wearing. "It's all right to laugh loudly. But we must talk quietly, so they think we're talking about *them*. Well, we are, sort of, since *we* know who wrote on the bathroom walls. . . . Now, go on—but softer."

"I'm sorry," I said.

"Don't be," answered Penny. "But wait—shut up— come with me. I have a new idea. A super one! It just came to me."

"What?" I asked, wondering how my head could ever take in a new strategy when I had just begun to understand "Ronald H. loves Noreen M."

As I was asking, I caught sight of Martha, clinging with both hands to the chain-link fence. She was all alone and staring off into space. Without stopping to think, I grabbed Penny's arm and said, "What about Martha? Shouldn't we ask her to help? Wouldn't three be better than two?" I said this because I remembered again how kind Penny had been to Martha on yesterday's field trip.

"No, no," Penny insisted, pulling me—since I still had hold of her arm—toward the yard bathroom marked *Girls*. "For this strategy, Pru, only two. Only two P's in a pod!"

It seemed as if I was spending practically my whole day in bathrooms, but I didn't mind because Penny's new strategy turned out to be so original. First, we changed shirts. I ended up wearing her blue-checked Levi shirt and she ended up with my flowered green one. Just trading, however, wasn't the original part. Putting them on *backward*—buttoning them all the way up the back so that from the front they looked like high turtlenecks—now, that was original. Even if the backward-buttoned collars choked us a little, it was worth it.

"Backward is chic," Penny kept telling me as we were laughing, helping each other button up, and admiring ourselves in the mirror.

While we were doing these things, we both noticed that the Book Squad had already been at work trying to remove "Ronald and Noreen" from the bathroom wall. The Book Squad, I ought to explain, is a special group of students (trustworthy ones) in charge of going through the bathrooms and halls at school and taking off the dirty words written on them. They're called the Book Squad because sometimes the only way to deal with a certain four-letter word beginning with *f*—if it has been written in indelible ink—is to write *over* it so that it says *book* instead of the *f*-word.

"Listen, Pru," Penny told me when we'd finished laughing about changing our shirts around, and about the work of the Book Squad, "I'm not at all sure about Harrington and Mrs. Monzoni. We may be all wrong. There may be something else going on. Something more complicated. So we may have to do a little spying. But first—look!"

Then, before I knew quite what was happening, Penny pulled a blue felt pen out of her pocket and, in large spidery script, *she* left a message on the bathroom wall.

As soon as she was finished writing, she ran out the door and began to shout toward the girls at Alyson's party.

"Come see," she was calling. "Come see what's on the bathroom wall now!"

Just reading it left me doubled over with a crazy case of giggles. Now, in curly blue letters, the wall said, "Ronald H. loves Cal Williams."

It was perfect—just perfect. First of all, any twelve-year-old boy who made a career of relieving himself against trees deserved to have his name written that way. Secondly, it was such a ridiculous thought that it would make *everyone* forget about Ronald and Noreen, giving Penny and me our chance to do some spying.

The third and best thing was that it completely broke up Alyson's party. Like a swarm of hornets, the girls deserted the south corner of the yard and came buzzing over to see what was on the wall. As they came, Penny and I in our backward shirts stood in the doorway like guards and, giggling, asked each girl to state her purpose for entering.

Most of them just said, "To see what's on the wall."

After a while, though, it all got a little silly because Janey Kline said she was coming in to "doodle," which made Kim Lytton say she was coming to "wee-wee."

Then the bathroom words got more and more vulgar, until most of us were standing around laughing at our own language and at the stupid idea that Mr. Harrington would even care if Cal Williams existed. We were kind of spread around with half of us inside the little lavatory and half of us outside—all talking at once. Penny and I were also busy, of course, explaining that we were wearing our shirts backward because it was chic.

By the time Alyson and Brooke—unable to stand being left out any longer—came, Penny and I were having our own un-birthday party. Laughing, we were passing out little bathroom cups full of water that everyone said was so much better tasting than Alyson's icky, too sweet red soda.

Alyson's face, as she marched toward us, looked almost as red as that soda. Red and angry in the middle of her head of orange-ish hair. The lobes of her ears were red, too, so red I could hardly see her little ladybug earrings. Brooke, the stringbean, was right behind her shoulder, scowling.

Before either of them could say a word, though, Penny rushed up to them swinging her hair. "Oh, Alyson—I feel so bad about interrupting your party, but the writing is so funny! And, Brooke—listen—about yesterday. I'm really sorry about that, but it just came to me that I *had* to do it. I thought if *I* got mad at you for being mean to Martha, I could save you. Save you from Harrington—and from having him have a fit and then lecturing you until we all turned into icicles on that stupid dune! I'm sorry, but I did it for *you*. Really I did!"

Like everything Penny came up with, that approach worked, too. Only a minute later, it seemed, Alyson and Brooke were smiling and drinking water out of our paper cups. Then, when the taste of soda was rinsed from their mouths, they actually took off their shirts and began buttoning them up backward just because Penny had told them it was chic.

"Why, everyone Back East—in New York and all—is wearing turned-around shirts," she was repeating as Martha appeared.

Suddenly all the noise and giggles were choked away as Martha, in a maroon leotard worn with her usual green skirt and ballet slippers, began to make her way into the bathroom. My stomach felt jumpy when I saw that her face looked as scared and custardy as it had yesterday on the school bus. She was probably unable to stay away any longer, I decided, because she was terrified that the something written on the bathroom wall was about her. Not that having her name on the wall would be anything unusual. In fact, it appeared there quite regularly as part of various kinds of insults.

Martha looked almost as if she were in pain—not too different from the way Harrington had looked this morning. I wanted to jump forward and protect her. But Penny didn't move from where she was standing next to me, so I didn't, either.

"What's the matter, Martha?" Alyson asked in a mean, teasing way.

"She's in a hurry to doodle," Janey Kline answered.

"No, no," Kim Lytton chimed in, ". . . to wee-wee!"

Ignoring the rising wave of giggles and silly laughter, Martha just pushed her way through all of us and locked herself into one of the stalls.

"No, no, no," Brooke said, standing on tiptoe to make sure her croaky voice carried over the top of the cubicle. "She's come to change her Kotex!"

I should have been brave then. Should have, all by myself, done what I knew was right. Should have told Brooke, as fiercely as Penny had told her the day before, to shut up and stop being so cruel. But, buttoned backward into Penny's shirt with the slightly choking collar, I was a mouse, a worm . . . a nerd.

I didn't know whether Martha had her period. I didn't even know if she'd started having them. All I knew was that Penny wasn't saying anything. And, hating myself, I didn't say anything either. Along with Penny and the others, I gave in to all my worst instincts. Then I, too, laughed at Martha, locked in the cubicle, who was—maybe—changing her Kotex. But maybe not.

FOR THE REST OF THE WEEK, I WAS FURIOUS WITH myself for not sticking up for Martha in the bathroom, and I kept thinking that Penny and I were about to have our first real argument. Real friends usually have real arguments. I knew that from Pittsburgh with Ruthie. (Sometimes she and I used to have terrible fights, but then, with a little help from her brother Milton, who never seemed to get angry about anything, we'd make up and be better friends than ever.)

The reason I thought Penny and I were going to fight

—at last—was very simple. We would not bother to fight over Martha and how she was being treated, but over *ear piercing*. The fight would happen because Penny, in her usual calm, friendly way, continued to remind me that Saturday we were both going to Littlefields to get our ears pierced.

"It's a seven-dollar special," she kept telling me, "for the piercing and the little solid-gold studs that stay in for four weeks."

It wasn't the money that was upsetting me. I still had a ten-dollar bill my grandmother had given me for Christmas. Nor was it the fact that I would be making my folks crazy-mad at me for doing such a thing when they had absolutely forbidden me to consider it. It was, however, because she—Penny—just *assumed* that I—Pru—would do it for no other reason than because *she* said so. Suddenly I was beginning to feel like a chicken's wishbone being pulled in two directions. Pulled between what *I* wanted to do and what *she* wanted me to do. Something was surely going to snap and when it did, for the first time in our five-week friendship, I was going to swing my hair and stomp my foot as I spoke to Penny. I was going to yell and scream and tell her that it was not Mom's decision or Dad's or *hers*. But mine. My head. My ears. My own ears that were about to have hurting, bloody little holes punched in them.

(I hate pain almost as much as I hate heights!) My earlobes! My poor, sensitive little pink earlobes!

But I never said any of those things to Penny. Not one of them. I was terrified of furious parents and of pain, but I was even more afraid of disappointing my friend. Besides, when the time came, she made everything so easy for me that I almost forgot I had meant to argue with her.

You see, I was only half awake on Saturday morning listening to the pickety-pickety-pick sound of Mom's typewriter in the living room below me (she was slaving over an article on "Herring in San Francisco Bay"), when Penny called me on the phone to invite me to her apartment for breakfast.

"Ma's making waffles," she explained, sounding impossibly wide-awake and energetic. "She and Father want to meet you—in the worst way. So get dressed, will you, and come now. But . . . be sure and bring your ten dollars."

Almost without thinking, I was pulling on my jeans, Penny's clogs, and buttoning up—backward, of course— my green flowered shirt. Then I was rushing through the house, kissing my mother, who hardly noticed because her head was swimming with herring, and patting Lion on the head when I noticed him sitting in Daddy's chair working on his latest junk sculpture.

Junk sculpture—collecting stuff and glueing it down on big boards then spray-painting it—was one of his hobbies.

"Say hi to Dad when he gets up," I said, glad that they were both too preoccupied to pay any attention to me. "See you later!"

I was heading toward the door when Mom stopped pecking at her typewriter. "Wait a minute," she called out, suddenly alert. "Did you say where you were going, Prudie? Did you? I thought you promised Daddy you'd help him finish that dragon kite today. . . ."

Before I could tell about being invited for waffles, Lion looked up from his junk and answered for me. "Penny, Penny," he insisted, rearranging the wild hair of his that I had dared to touch. "If Pru is running off without breakfast after a telephone call, it must have something to do with Penny. She must be going to meet Penny! Hey, can I come along?"

Thanks to Lion, I was held up and had to waste several precious minutes, while I hopped from foot to foot, doing my explaining to him and to Mom. They kept trying to get at me by bringing up the subject of that stupid kite again. Just because Dad and I liked reading better than making things with our hands, Mom and Lion had bought us a complicated Chinese dragon kite to "have fun assembling." Some fun. Between us, my father and I had twenty thumbs, and I knew that even if the kite ever got pieced, tied, and glued together, it would never fly. Mom and Lion simply couldn't seem to accept the fact that I was happier reading romantic books and Dad was happier burying himself in archaeological studies of earlier, pre-smog civilizations.

Finally, though, by promising to return in the early afternoon, so Dad and I could continue our kite-making adventure, I managed to escape. Then, at last, I was hurrying off to Penny's apartment, listening to the clopping sound her blue clogs made against the grainy sidewalk, and listening, also, to the crisp ten-dollar bill as it crackled faintly in my front pocket. I couldn't wait to get to Penny's. I couldn't wait.

But, you know—to tell the truth—I could have waited even longer. After all the weeks of being excited, of imagining her parents and her apartment, being there wasn't such a big deal. It was a nice enough place but not chic. It had the usual assortment of couches, comfortable chairs, lamps, and tables. There were a few pictures, also, and a few tired-looking plants.

The Hoffmans were nice enough, at least to me and Penny. But they, like their plants, were kind of wilted and tired-looking. Neither one seemed to notice that Penny and I looked alike. Or if they noticed, they didn't think it was important enough to mention. They were too busy, it seemed, looking at one another over the plates of waffles (good, but not as good as my mother's) in such a way that I almost thought I could see daggers shooting out of their eyes at one another, like you see sometimes in cartoons.

The invisible daggers, Penny explained the moment we left her apartment on our way to Littlefields, were flying through the air because her mother had just caught her father smoking in the bathroom again. While the water in the shower ran and ran as though he had been taking one, he had been sitting on the closed toilet puffing on cigarettes. One after another, until Mrs. Hoffman had sprung the lock on the door, opened it, and caught him.

"He's killing himself," Penny explained, looking about a hundred times as serious as she usually did. "People with emphysema just *can't* smoke. It will kill him, and Ma doesn't even know where he gets the cigarettes, since he can hardly breathe well enough to walk across the street, much less to the corner store."

I think I chattered a lot on the bus as we rode downtown. I was trying to make Penny feel more cheerful and trying not to wonder how such worn-down, ordinary people could possibly be the parents of a sparkling, original person like Penny. I also talked and talked so I wouldn't have any time to feel sorry for my ear-lobes.

About the ear-piercing itself, the less said the better. The man doing it looked like some half-mad Dr. Frankenstein. He was only an earring salesman, for heaven's sake, yet he wore a scary-looking starched white coat. He had a table full of stuff, too. Alcohol, cotton swabs, files, ointments, and something black that looked like a gun. Then Penny and I had to stand in line, looking at that coat and the other junk, watching him grin as he stabbed into all the ears lined up in front of us.

"What if . . . ," I asked Penny, beginning to feel a little sick and shaky, ". . . he saves all the holes he punches out and pieces them together to make wallets and lampshades?"

"Shut up," Penny said sweetly. "Think of something else. Something fascinating like Harrington."

Instead of listening to her suggestion, I clutched at her arm and began pleading with her. "You go first, Penny, please. Please—while I *think* about it."

"Of course," she answered. "And don't worry about permission slips either. I've got them. . . ."

And she did. When our turn came, she eased herself into the hard chair, produced a pair of signed permission slips, and let that man operate on her. She didn't even make a face as he pinched something and left her earlobes marked with shiny little balls. I wasn't quite so calm, however. Someone—Penny, maybe— pushed me down into the chair and held me there. Even with my eyes closed, I sat on the edge of the seat, wriggling and jerking against the hands that were holding on to me. As I sat, I could hear someone, who might have been me, crying out like a baby.

Then the next thing I knew, my eyes were open and that creepy man was grabbing my money, giving me the change, and pushing me out of the chair. As if he didn't care about me or care that my tender earlobes had ugly holes through them now, he stared past me and in his oozy voice said, "Next!"

During the whole process, I never looked at the instrument he used. Not straight on, anyway. Nor was there any pain I can remember. The pain was in my stomach instead of my ears. All over again, as my ears were being mutilated, I was furious with myself for not having argued with Penny, for having allowed *her* to make up *my* mind. As I had—without a whimper— allowed her to decide for me yesterday that I wouldn't stick up for Martha in the yard bathroom. . . .

But by the time I began to get really worked up, it was all over and Penny and I were standing together by the elevator, looking at our earlobes in a display mirror. As we were examining how they were dotted with gold studs, I suddenly realized, for the first time, that Penny had strategies for me, too. Not just for other people. Today's strategy, for instance, had been to distract me with waffles and emphysema until I didn't have time to remember I was not going to let anyone put holes through my ears.

Instead of getting mad, though, I surprised myself by smiling happily at the girl in the mirror, who smiled back at me. I had wanted for years—even in Pittsburgh with Ruthie—to have my ears pierced. Now, thanks to Penny, it was done. Her strategy had been for my own good. It had helped me get over all my fears about my parents and about the pain. I had at last been totally independent. Done something—something important to me—that I'd been afraid of doing for much too long.

"Thanks," I whispered to her as we stood there side by side, looking terribly alike in the mottled depart-ment-store mirror.

I wasn't the only one excited to have gone through with the piercing. Penny was super-happy, too, and all the way back on the bus we both kept reaching up to touch where the studs were poking through our ears. And we talked about what we were supposed to do to take care of them. (Penny had listened to the man's instructions, even if I hadn't: alcohol three times

a day and twist the little gold balls to prevent infec-
tions.) We also talked about earrings—what kind we'd
buy in four weeks when we could remove the studs.

"I'll buy you a pair," Penny told me, "and you'll buy
me one. But *not alike*. Then we'll trade one each—so
we will each have a different earring in each ear. Now
that will be really chic!"

Backward shirts had been all right with me, but I
wasn't sure about wearing non-matching earrings. That
sounded peculiar—even a little nerdy. "What if . . . ,"
I began asking myself, "we end up having our first big
argument over the earrings, instead of over having
holes put in my ears?"

I didn't bring up the subject, though. I just nodded
and followed Penny off the bus at the stop near school.
"Let's check on the action over in the yard," she suggested.

"Okay," I agreed, knowing that the action in the
schoolyard on any Saturday wouldn't interest me in
the least—and knowing I should go right home to face
my family.

But, still, I went along with Penny, walked until we
came to Harrington's Chevy, and peered into the yard.
The only action going on there was a sweaty three-on-
three game of basketball being played by Cal Williams
and some of his friends.

"What a bore," Penny said, sighing.

I was just about to agree with her, when—all of a sudden—Penny grabbed my arm. "Duck," she whispered.
"Behind the car."

"Why?" I asked.

"No—don't duck," she said, changing her mind so
quickly she left me half standing and half bent. "Let's
just lean back against the fence. Just lean here."

"Why?" I asked again.

"Because," she explained patiently. "Look—here
comes Martha."

.7.

YES, THERE SHE WAS—MARTHA BRANDEBERRY, THE CLASS nerd, out for a Saturday stroll. In a blue leotard and the usual skirt and shoes, with her purse over her shoulder, she was coming up the other side of the street. Clutched tightly against her chest was a manila envelope. If she saw us (and how could she miss seeing two look-alike classmates with newly pierced ears bouncing their bottoms against the chain-link fence and staring over at her), she chose to pretend we didn't exist. I was about to call out, thinking Penny might want to use this opportunity to pump her for information again.

But, suddenly, Penny squeezed my elbow. "No," she whispered. "She's going to Harrington's! And we're going to spy!"

Penny was absolutely right. Martha *was* going to Harrington's. She stopped at the front door of his building only long enough to press his bell and wait for his buzzer to release the lock. Then she slipped in the front door and disappeared.

Instead of waiting where we were, I followed Penny as she bolted across the street and pushed his bell exactly as Martha had done. Again, from somewhere up on the third floor, he used his buzzer, only this time it was the two P's who slipped in. Martha didn't see us, though, because she was already running up the second flight of stairs. We didn't follow her. Penny gestured and held on to my elbow until I understood that we were going to wait in the lobby, just listening to her ballet slippers pitty-patting above us.

I wanted to climb the stairs, too, quietly—staying just a little way behind Martha. But I knew Penny was right to insist that we stay down where we were safe. We couldn't see, but we'd listen. Find out if Martha went into his flat. Find out how long she stayed.

My heart was knocking against my ribs. "What if

. . . Mrs. Monzoni is there and Martha catches them together half dressed?" I whispered to Penny.

"Ssh, Pru. Ssh!" she answered, putting a hand across my mouth and looking as if I'd said something very, very funny.

When Martha's soft steps stopped, we could hear a faint knock and a door opening. We could hear voices, too, Harrington's and hers.

"Come on in," he said, his voice echoing through the tiled stairwell. "How come you rang twice? You never do that."

"I didn't," Martha told him. "Only once."

Of course, she hadn't rung twice. The second ring had been Penny's. I was beginning to get very nervous, when—after a moment of silence—Harrington spoke again. "Come in," he repeated.

Well, one thing was certain. Mrs. Monzoni wasn't there, or he wouldn't be inviting Martha Brandeberry into his flat. Maybe, I decided, he'd asked Martha to stop by so they could talk privately about who had been writing such awful things about him on the bathroom walls.

"Come in," he repeated for the third time.

"I can't," Martha said, in a voice so thin I could hardly hear it. "But there are the poems. And that article. All typed and proofread. I hope they're neat enough. I'm having some problems with my aunt's typewriter."

"What kind?" he asked.

"Of what?" she asked, sounding like a total dummy.

"Of problems with your typewriter?" he answered, sounding vaguely annoyed at her for being so thick.

"Oh, that. Well . . . skipping mostly. The A particularly, and there just seem to be so many words with A's in them."

Penny and I could hear Harrington chuckle in response to this brilliant observation of hers. "Yes . . . yes—lots of A's, I'm afraid. Well, look—if you can't come in—just wait and let me get the other stuff for you."

I poked at Penny. I had heard enough, and I wanted to get out before Martha came tippy-toeing down the stairs and found us there. We were terrific spies. We had just managed to find out what absolutely everyone already knew. Big stuff. So nerdy Martha made a little money typing things for Harrington. The only original information we'd come up with was that she used her aunt's typewriter and that its A's were skipping.

"He must be getting her her money," I whispered to Penny. "The least she could do with it is buy herself a new skirt. Come on—let's go!"

Penny didn't move. With that secretive smile that always got to me, she shook her head and motioned for me to join her over in the dark, dusty corner behind the stairway. Then we waited.

After a minute or two, Harrington said, "Here—and thank you, Martha."

She should have said, "You're welcome," or something like that, but she didn't. She said, "I'm working on the adjectives," which from where I was crouching didn't make any sense at all. In fact, I had to bite down on my hand to keep from giggling, and I didn't dare look over at Penny.

If they said anything else to one another up there—even good-by—we never heard it. After a few more seconds of high-above-us foot-shuffling, Harrington's door slammed and Martha's feet began to tap lightly down the stairs.

When she reached the lobby, she could have seen us there behind the stairway. If she'd only twisted her head a quarter of a turn, we'd have been clearly visible. But she didn't. With her lips held stiffly together, she just rushed right past us, opened the door, and was gone.

"Whee!" Penny squealed softly as soon as we were alone. "We were in luck today! Were we in luck!"

"Mmm," I agreed, wondering how Penny's enthusiasm could extend to finding out secrets we already knew.

"Now," she said, suddenly quite willing to go up the

stairs, "let's see if there's a door to the roof. We've got to do some more spying. Let's see if that outside fire escape goes down right by his window. Or let's just ring the bell and test Harrington by telling him *we've* come to talk about who wrote on the walls."

"No," I answered, surprising myself by daring to go against Penny's wishes. It wasn't easy, either—especially when she was burning up with that fiery energy of hers. But my ears were beginning to hurt.

"What did you say?" she asked.

"I'm sorry, Penny. Really, I'm sorry, but no. Not today. No, I just can't. I've got to see my parents. Tell them—you know—*confess* about my ears. I'm going to have to listen to them explode, and it's going to be just too much if I . . . and besides, there's this stupid kite I'm supposed to . . . well, listen, Penny, I'm sorry, but . . . ."

"Don't be," Penny answered, patting me on the back as she watched the tears that were beginning to leak out of the corners of my eyes. "It's okay. Don't worry, Pru. Why, we have all kinds of time. Next week —any week—to work on our strategy. Don't worry, Pru. It's okay. Everything is okay!"

With Penny's comforting words still ringing in my ears, I left her there in Harrington's lobby and ran all the way home. Then, thinking like Penny, feeling like

Penny, and acting like her, too, I threw myself, sobbing, into my mother's arms.

"Oh, Mom! Mommy!" I kept crying, hugging and clutching on to her. "I did a terrible, terrible thing. My ears, Mommy. They've been pierced. I was awful and sneaky and I'm sorry—so sorry. Sorry . . . sorry . . . sorry!"

I was only half conscious that my dad and Lion were there watching and listening to me bawl and babble. They weren't saying anything, just sitting there like a small audience at some very, very dramatic play.

Mom, I think, was crying, too—all emotional as she told me how *disappointed* she was, how I had let her down by doing something I'd been forbidden to do. But after several minutes, when I was just beginning to run out of apologies and tears, I realized that she had begun to come around. Now she was holding my shaking body, hugging it and whispering soothing words into my mutilated ears.

"Don't cry, honey baby. Don't. We didn't want you to do it, but what's done is done. I'm disappointed— yes, I am, but it doesn't look too bad. Does it, Irv?" she asked, turning back toward my father.

Not too many minutes later, we were all sitting on the couch—the four of us—while I tried to calm down and stop hiccupping as Mom, Dad, and Lion each

examined my tender earlobes. It was a nice family scene,
I was thinking, as I wiped at my eyes with my dad's
pocket handkerchief and looked over at the mantel
with its row of beautiful painted eggs and then back at
the copper disc of peacock fragments hanging around
my mother's neck. At that moment, I was only partly
aware that I'd created this lovely scene by using a
Penny-like strategy.

Then, all of a sudden, my dad got up, moved to his
big easy chair, and said something that snapped me
out of my comfortable, dreamy happiness. "I think I've
had just about enough of Penny Hoffman," he told me.

"What?" my voice cried out.

"I think I've had enough of Penny Hoffman," he repeated, enunciating distinctly.

"Penny?" I gasped. "But she's my friend. My *best*
friend. I thought you liked her!"

Slowly, my dad nodded. "I did. I do. But something's
wrong, Pru. She's keyed you up—made you very hyper
and headstrong. There's something wrong, and I . . . ."

"I know what it is. I know," Lion shrieked, interrupting what sounded like the beginning of a long, exhausting lecture. "See—there—that's what's wrong. Prudie's
left ear. See, the little gold thing—it's not in the middle
like the one on the right. It's off-center—way off-center.
At least a millimeter. Look, look!"

"Shut up," I told him, jumping up from my perch on the arm of the couch. When I said "shut up," I really said it, too. With a yell. Not nice and considerate-sounding as if it were coming out of Penny's mouth, but mad and ugly.

I could see Mom, with Penny's disc swinging on its ribbon, reaching out to squeeze Daddy's hand, hoping to quiet him down so he wouldn't keep on hurting my feelings. Dad, however, didn't pay any attention to her. He just kept his eyes—eyes clear of weekday smog—on my face. When he spoke again, his voice was low and even. It wasn't mean or angry—just very serious. "She worries me, that Penny," he said. "I always have the feeling that with her, you're only as good as your last deal."

I wasn't exactly sure what he meant—only sure I didn't like it. Not at all, and I wasn't going to listen to another word against her. No one—not even my own father—could say bad things about Penny. Could say that with her I was only as good as my last deal!

Turning my back, I ran up the stairs two by two and slammed into my bedroom. Then I just stayed there, for hours it seemed, all alone—staring at myself in the mirror. Staring and thinking how difficult it was for unusual, distinctive people like Penny and me to live with ordinary, unspectacular families.

As I stood there staring and thinking, I couldn't help noticing that Lion (blast his IQ) had been right about the off-center left stud. "But I can fix it," I told myself comfortingly. "I'll pull on it, when it stops throbbing—stretch the lobe out so it evens up. I can do that. I can. . . ."

Then feeling better, I stood there looking at my full, shining black hair, my green eyes, my backward shirt, and my earlobes, and thinking how chic I'd look—Penny and I both—when we were able to put real earrings into them. A different earring for each lobe, too. Brooke and Alyson would be so jealous. I couldn't wait.

THE HANDWRITING WAS ON THE WALLS THE WEEK AFTER
Penny and I had our ears pierced and spied on Harrington. It was on the ceilings, too, and even on the
floors of all the girls' bathrooms and boys' bathrooms at
Portola Hill. Like weird, exotic flowers, "love" burst
into multicolored bloom all over those lavatories. If
"loves" were being written on the walls of the ones
used by our teachers, they never told us. It didn't really
matter, though, because we were having so much fun.
What had started the week before as a minor dribble

of bathroom insults and accusations had suddenly turned into a happening. Not only was it hilarious, but it helped me to forget what my father had said about Penny.

Monday, Tuesday, Wednesday, Thursday, Friday. Each day new "loves" in more original colored inks in different handwritings appeared on the walls. "Ronald H. loves Noreen M." (an oldie but goodie) was one of the first to appear, closely followed by "Ronald H. loves Myrtle K." and "Ronald loves himself." (Myrtle K., as we call her, or Miss Kremenski, is the other sixth-grade homeroom teacher and not exactly, at age sixty (about), the kind of ravishing female Harrington might be expected to pursue.)

After those first few "loves," the handwriting went crazy. "Ronald H. loves Cal" came back, along with "Ronald H. loves his Chevy." Also, "Ronald H. loves the sixth-grade girls" and "Ronald H. loves the sixth-grade boys." Another one said, "Noreen M. loves Ronald H. and Mr. M." Then the accusations began to branch out. Someone wrote, "Brooke loves Alyson," and someone else scribbled, "Cal loves Pru." "P. loves P." showed up, too. Etcetera. Etcetera.

According to the boys, whose bathrooms we didn't see, their walls said all the same things, only a little more crudely, since the f-word was used there most of the time in place of "loves." More and more names kept appearing in sillier and sillier combinations—including a lot of movie-star names, too, such as "Ronald H. loves Robert Redford" and "Ronald loves Tatum O'Neal"—so it didn't bother me to have my name or Penny's up there with all the others.

By Wednesday, the Book Squad gave up entirely. There was, they decided, no use cleaning the walls because the minute something was scrubbed away, it would reappear, written twice or three times instead of only once. Never had the bathrooms at Portola Hill had so much use. A stranger visiting the school would have thought we had all come down with some rare East African bladder disease.

And still, the phantom writing went on. I say "phantom" because no one ever admitted actually seeing anyone write anything. As if by some kind of spontaneous magic, the accusations kept spreading wider and wider—until Friday. Friday someone, using ink the color of green corduroy, wrote "Ronald H. loves Martha" and "Martha loves Ronald H." That was predictable, too, as it had been predictable that someone would call Martha an elephant seal. By Friday, though, no one cared. At least, no one but Mrs. Monzoni, Harrington, and the other teachers.

They were grim-faced, as they had been all week.

While the fourth and fifth graders continued to giggle and peek wide-eyed into the bathrooms, the teachers treated us—the sixth graders—as if we had some serious but not fatal disease. We would recover, they hinted by their unsmiling but fairly tolerant treatment. They had decided, evidently, that instead of being *discussed*, the disease had to be allowed to run its course.

At home that week, where I was trying to spend as little time as possible, I was being handled the same way. My family were nice—always nice—but they kept giving me strange, anxious looks. No one said a word, good or bad, about Penny—and no one mentioned ears or the alcohol-soaked wads of cotton piling up in the bathroom wastebasket, either. The only clue to the way my nice, nice family was feeling was that Daddy stayed downtown late two nights in a row, while Mom stopped typing, skipped her writers' class, and began painting three goose eggs to look like medieval stained-glass windows. Even Lion didn't say anything unpleasant. Once or twice, I caught him—looking up from the dragon kite, which he had decided only he was brilliant enough to assemble—staring at my left ear where the stud was, as he had said, at least a millimeter closer to my cheek. But he didn't make a single comment.

I was so excited by everything going on at school that my cheeks began to flush a beautiful pink—just the way Penny's always did. If my family noticed my pretty cheeks, they didn't say anything, and so I didn't tell them about the bathroom walls. At first I didn't tell because they didn't *ask* if anything exciting was happening at school. Then, later, I didn't because they—like my teachers—were acting as if my cheeks were flushed because of some unmentionable disease.

I didn't care, though. I wasn't having just a good week—but a fantastic one. Not only were Brooke and Alyson friendly with Penny and me, but because of the writing everybody seemed to like everybody. Except, of course, Martha. She simply avoided the bathrooms and the rest of us as though she thought our disease was the bubonic plague. It was really too bad she felt that way because that crazy week, even Martha could have felt popular and unnerdy.

Penny was using a special strategy to keep the excitement going, but oddly enough it had nothing to do with writing on walls. In fact, neither she nor I was doing any of the felt-pen writing. It was continuing to appear without our help. By mutual agreement, we took only pencils to school that week. What she—and then I, following her lead—*did* do was drop a lot of secret hints.

"We're onto something big—really big," Penny kept whispering to Alyson, Brooke, and a few of the others.

"About Harrington. Not just jokes for the wall, but the real stuff. We're spying. And soon—soon we'll know. But—ssh!—don't say anything. As soon as we know for sure, we'll tell." As Penny talked, with her cheeks rosy and hair swinging, she'd keep fingering the little gold studs in her ears.

So I did the same thing—swung my hair, twisted the studs, and whispered about how we were spying and would have IMPORTANT THINGS TO TELL. I didn't really believe what I was saying, but I had faith in Penny. If she was insisting we were onto something big, I trusted her. When the time came, she would let me know, and together we would share in the excitement. We were, after all, the two P's. Two P's in a pod.

All week, I was half expecting Harrington to come and drag me back into the men's room for another anxious, private chat, but he didn't. The only private chats I had that week were with Penny. As we laughed, fingered our earlobes, wore our shirts backward and traded off clothes, she kept telling me that *Saturday* would be the day. The big day to find out.

Last Saturday—Ear-Piercing Saturday—I had dreaded terribly. But I was almost crazy with excitement looking forward to this one. I, like everyone else, wanted to know the real truth about Ronald B. Harrington, Portola Hill's True Man of Mystery. Not only did I want to know, but—along with Penny—I wanted to be able to swing my hair and have the importance of being a leader and telling all of the sixth grade exactly what we knew. Only once or twice as I looked forward to Spying Saturday did I remember my bathroom talk with Harrington and how moved I'd been to see the desperate look in his deep-set eyes. I preferred to keep thinking about Penny and me. About Saturday morning, when we were going to meet behind the yew tree that grew by the front door of Harrington's apartment building.

At last *the day* came. Leaving a note saying I was going to Penny's, I slipped out before anyone was up. It was a gray, foggy morning—the kind of San Francisco day when maybe it would rain and maybe it wouldn't. Even in my warm patchwork sweater and with Penny's coiling scarf around my head and ears, I was shivering as I hurried to meet my friend behind the yew. "Maybe," I told myself, "I'm just shaking with excitement. Nothing—nothing, not even fog, is going to ruin this day for me." As I was saying these things to myself and cutting through the park, I caught sight of Cal Williams standing by a big pine tree.

He wasn't performing his usual disgusting act, probably because he'd already finished. As I saw him notice me, I thought he seemed to be adjusting and locking the top of his zipper.

"Where are you going, Pru?" he asked in that gruff, twelve-year-old voice of his. "To do some spying, huh?"

I glared at him. As I did, I knew Penny wouldn't have glared. She'd have flashed him a blinding, secretive smile. But as far as I was concerned, Cal Williams was still Cal Williams and didn't deserve a smile of any kind as he stood near the tree leering at me with a Huck Finn-ish grin. Leering with his tanned, just-beginning-to-pimple face. Anyway, it made me furious to think that *he* would know I was going spying. After all, Penny and I hadn't told very many people besides Brooke and Alyson, and we had sworn everyone to secrecy.

"Going spying on Harrington?" he asked when I failed to answer his first question. "And how come alone? I thought it was always the two P's—Penny and Prudie—together!"

"Shut up," I told him, using the tone of voice I usually reserved for Lion. No one, except Mom or Dad, was allowed to call me "Prudie." I loathed that nickname the way Lion hated having his hair rumpled, and Cal knew it because I'd screamed at him about it at least a thousand times.

"Prudie . . . Prudie baby—are you going off to do

the dirty work for Penny? Are you, huh? She's sending *you* off to snoop while she stays home where it's safe, Prudie?"

"Shut up!" I yelled at him. "Shut up! Shut your big, fat, ugly face, you stupid nerd. Shut up! Shut up! Shut up!"

It felt wonderful to be screeching at him that way—partly because it was Cal, but partly because I suddenly realized that ever since I'd met Penny on Harrington's fender, I hadn't yelled at anyone. (Not even Lion, really.) Penny didn't yell, so I didn't, either. But I liked to yell. It made me feel good and, on a morning when I was already feeling weirdly excited, yelling made me feel even better. In fact, I was bursting with such energy that in my excitement, I followed the "shut-ups" with a few more choice expressions—including ones that used the *f*-word. I told him to *f* off and I called him a name. A name that fitted him perfectly. A disgusting, seven-letter one that started with *A*.

That did it. After hearing that from my mouth, he took off through the park as if he was being chased by a mad, biting dog. Watching him go, I smiled happily to myself. Then I turned and hurried on to meet Penny who, I knew, was already waiting. She was. She had all the strategy mapped out, too. All I had to do was follow.

First we pressed Harrington's bell and waited for him to push the buzzer to unlock the door. Then we quickly let ourselves in and crouched down under the stairwell.

"Breathe quietly," Penny whispered, calling attention to the fact that I was actually panting with anticipation.

As we waited under the stairs, we could hear a door opening up on the third floor. Then there was about half a minute of scary silence. Next we heard Harrington's voice. "Who's there? Anybody there?"

Leaning against one another, trying not to move an inch, Penny and I waited.

"Hey," he shouted down. "I said—is anybody there?" Again he waited for an answering voice or any clue that someone was below.

After another long minute of no sound except for the thump of my heart playing a bongo rhythm somewhere deep inside my chest, we could hear him speaking again. "Oh, hell," he muttered. "Kids again. I hate 'em!" Then he slammed his door.

Straining to be quiet, Penny and I collapsed on the floor giggling. "So he hates kids, does he?" Penny said, rolling over and sitting up again. "Well, we shall see. . . ."

"What?" I asked, pulling myself up to a sitting position and trying to figure out what complicated thoughts were spinning around behind Penny's shining green eyes.

"To the roof," she said in a trembly whisper. "That's our stake-out position."

"The roof?" I gasped.

"Ssh!" she cautioned.

"I'm sorry."

"Don't be," she told me, jumping to her feet in one swift, graceful motion. As she reached down and pulled me up by her side, she spoke again. "Stake-out," she hissed. "On the roof. Up there we can talk. Now, come on!"

Because she smiled and spoke with such a wonderful rush of confidence, I did as she said. Moving slowly, we tried to climb the stairs without a sound. Once we had to leap back and press our bodies against the stairway wall because we thought we heard the tenant on the second floor about to open the door. But he (or she) didn't. Otherwise our trip up the four flights of stairs leading to the trap door that opened out onto the roof was totally uneventful.

Before I quite knew what I had done, I had helped Penny push up the trap door and she and I were standing on Harrington's roof—three whole stories above the street and sidewalk. Only then—a bit late—did I realize that this was not exactly the place for me.

"I think I'm going to vomit," I told Penny as we knelt

and eased the trap door quietly back into place.

"No, you won't," she answered, patting me comfortingly on one shoulder. "You'll get used to it. Mind over matter. Besides, this is the *only* way to the fire escape—the one that goes down right past Harrington's window. I checked it all out last Saturday, you know, after you went home to face your folks."

"Mmm," I answered, trying to be courageous and not pay attention to the fact that I was so choked up I couldn't swallow.

Cars were driving by below us on Portola. Looking down at them made me very dizzy. Afraid, I clutched at the metal handle of the trap door.

"Lie down," Penny suggested softly. "Flat—you'll feel better. We may have a long time to wait."

"For what?" I asked, as I allowed Penny to help me stretch out on the tar paper and gravel roof. Even stretched out, I didn't seem to feel any better. So I lay there, still clinging to that firm metal handle. If I hadn't felt so weak, I might have yelled at Penny as I had yelled at Cal. I hated heights and had never in my whole life been on a roof before. But because of her, I was on a roof—a roof that didn't even have an edge around it! It was just a big, flat black roof with sprinkles of gravel.

"Don't panic," Penny said, using her gentlest voice.

"Just relax. You can stay here, and I'll be the lookout up in front."

"For what?" I asked again, aware of the disagreeably whiny tone in my voice. Why couldn't I *ever* understand Penny's strategies?

"For someone to come visit him."

"Who?" I asked.

Penny touched one earlobe and looked down to where I lay with the sharp gravel poking into my body. "Who knows?" she answered. "Whoever visits Ronald H. on Saturdays."

"But what if no one comes?"

"If no one comes—no one comes. We just go home and try again next week," she said. "And look—it's good and foggy, too. No one will notice us up here on a foggy day. But . . . it is sort of cold, Pru, and you're lying down out of the wind. Could I borrow your sweater? Trade it for my nylon shell before I go forward to look?"

Needless to say, I traded her my sweater for her lightweight shell. As I did, I noticed that she was wearing her shirt (well, not hers, really—my flowered one) buttoned frontward instead of backward. "She must have forgotten," I told myself as I watched her slipping into my bright patchwork sweater and beginning to crawl forward, using her elbows like a soldier on patrol, to the very front of the roof.

Deep down, though, I knew she hadn't forgotten. Penny didn't forget things. She'd done it on purpose, but I wouldn't call her back to ask her why. If I did, she'd smile and say something perky like "Backward all the time really isn't chic. Backward only *some* of the time—now, that's really classy!"

Thinking about shirts—backward or forward—and about strategies, I lay there so long I felt as if I was turning into a Hunchback-of-Notre-Dame-type gargoyle carved out of cold, dead stone. I don't know how long we waited, but to me it seemed like hours. Up ahead of me Penny, looking very much alive and totally fearless, was lying on the tar and gravel, leaning her elbows right over the edge of the roof as she kept watch.

Because we were much too far apart to talk during those long, draggy minutes, I tried to make the time go by by doing some what-iffing about Harrington. After all, it wasn't every day I had a chance to discover the truth about a Man of Mystery.

Even reminding myself how worked up I'd been this very morning, when I'd had the misfortune of coming across Cal Williams as he was zipping his pants, didn't work, though. I simply couldn't make myself concentrate on Harrington. Instead, every what-if I came up with, as I lay there freezing and being stabbed by a million pellets of loose gravel, had to do with my family.

"What if . . . I was home eating some of Mom's waffles? Or watching her fill in the tiny triangles of color on her stained-glass goose eggs while we talked about *Anna Karenina*. What if . . . Lion and I were doing a jigsaw together? Or I was helping him spray-paint his new junk sculpture? What if . . . my ears didn't have aching holes in them and I was sitting my too-big self in Daddy's lap laughing at his jokes and making him laugh about the writing on the walls at Portola Hill, while we both *refused* to work on that stupid kite?"

If Penny had been lying closer to me, I knew things would have been different. I would have caught some of her excitement. She would have smiled and encouraged me to stop thinking about my family and to start feeling as wildly curious as she did to find out about Harrington and . . . .

"Martha!" Penny said suddenly, her stage-whispery voice cutting right into my self-pitying gloom. "It's Martha, Pru. Martha! She's coming to see Harrington!"

As she was speaking, she scampered swiftly back to where I lay, still anchoring myself by clutching the handle of the trap door. She was sitting next to me then, and she began tugging to make me sit up.

"Now," she said. "Now we climb—quietly—down the fire escape so we can see what happens when Martha goes in to see him!"

My body was limp and very heavy as Penny tried to pull me over to the edge of the big metal fire escape cage. Martha visiting Harrington was, as far as I was concerned, no big deal. She was obviously coming—just as she had last Saturday—to deliver some more papers she'd typed. My uncooperative body was telling me I didn't have to endanger my life and risk getting caught spying only to find out if the *A* on Martha's aunt's typewriter had been repaired so it didn't skip.

But Penny just wouldn't leave me alone. "Come on, Pru. Hurry! We don't want to miss out on anything. Listen, they have a *thing* going between them—Martha and Ronald! Now, we're going down the fire escape to look in through the curtains—and they're thin curtains —I checked last week—to see what they *do together*. But hurry—hurry—hurry!"

For once, her words seemed to have no effect on me at all. I shook my head. "I can't," I mumbled, holding the trap door handle even more tightly. "Too high and I'm afraid. I can't. . . ."

"Yes," she urged, "you can. But now—quickly—before she rings and gets in and up to his flat. We must position ourselves first so we won't get caught."

"No," I repeated stubbornly.

"Yes—yes. Look—the fire escape—it's all barred, all closed in. You can't possibly fall. Why, if you think about it for even a second, you'll know it's even safer than the roof!"

Feeling tears stinging in my eyes, I shook my head again. I wasn't sure, at that point, whether I was having an attack of terror or of conscience. But—whatever—I wasn't about to move.

"No," I said. "I can't. I'm sorry . . . sorry . . . oh, I'm so sorry, Penny . . . sorry, sorry. . . ."

"Don't be!" Penny told me, suddenly totally friendly and understanding. "I'll go down and watch. If you can just get yourself to crawl to the edge—where you'll have the fire escape bars to hang on to—then I'll be able to whisper to you and tell you all about it."

"Whisper? Whisper? They'll hear you. What if we get caught?"

"So what?" Penny said, smiling as she began easing herself down the fire escape. "They're the ones who will be embarrassed. Not us!"

Penny's irresistible persuasiveness. That's how I happened to find myself lying at the side edge of Ronald Harrington's roof, my hands gripping the top bars of his fire escape, as Penny sat ten feet below me peering into his living room window.

"He's heading toward the door," she whispered. "Martha must have rung already. He's standing there by the door—it's still closed—and he's waiting, pulling at his beard."

Despite my so-recent attack of fear and/or conscience, I couldn't help but notice that a curious, creepy-crawly feeling was beginning to run along my scalp and down the back of my neck. Martha wasn't even inside Harrington's apartment yet, and I could already see them together. I could see him sitting on a couch next to her, looking at her with his troubled eyes. That look couldn't help but affect a dreamy nerd like Martha Brandeberry. I mean, for someone like Martha, who had no one to love her except an aunt with a defective typewriter and an old grandmother (leaving out, of course, those parents of hers who hardly ever, according to my mom, showed up to even say hello), his look would be totally irresistible! Penny had seen that right from the first.

Penny had known the day of the elephant seals—or maybe even before that. And I hadn't really believed it even when their names were written in corduroy-green ink on the bathroom walls. Now though, I understood at last that all of Penny's strategies had been directed toward catching them together, and I wished I was scrunched down next to her where I, too, could see them.

"Penny," I said, keeping my voice as low as possible while I leaned my head and shoulders farther over the top of the fire escape steps. "Maybe I will come down." Somehow I wasn't as frightened of the height as I had been before.

"No," she warned me softly, "too late. He's opening the door. Ssh!"

Disappointed but knowing she was right, I edged forward a little more, looking down at my patchwork sweater and the top of Penny's dark head. As I looked, that strange feeling shivered through me again because I felt the way I'd felt weeks ago when I saw Penny hugging my mother. I felt, in some incredibly weird way, as if I was watching *myself* about to see the scene that was going to take place between Harrington and

Martha. But I wasn't. I was still up on the cold, gravelly roof. Because I wasn't as quick-thinking or brave as my friend, I had been left behind while she was about to see *everything*.

My body had been disappointingly slow. My mind, too. But now it, at least, was all revved up as I waited for more breathy whisperings from Penny. It was racing as fast as my heart into a whole fantastic series of what-ifs.

"What if . . . they sit together on the couch? What if . . . he looks at her as he looked at me—only harder and more romantically? What if . . . he reaches out and takes her hand? No, no—just *touches* it, first. Sort of brushes against it as he reaches for . . . for some of his papers? No, wait—not her hand. Her *foot*. His foot will touch her foot—her foot in the ballet slipper—just a tiny little touch, almost as if by accident. . . ."

I was getting completely carried away, and Penny hadn't said a thing. Not one thing. She was just hunched over at the edge of the window watching while I was imagining Martha and Harrington acting just like the characters in some of the books I'd read. A little bit of *Anna Karenina* or *Green Mansions* or *Jane Eyre*. Even a little bit of *Gone with the Wind*. (I hadn't read that one but had seen the movie—a movie so old it was made the year my father was born!)

"No, no . . . ," I told myself, reconsidering my last what-if. "Harrington's not the foot-touching type. More direct. What if . . . without saying a word, he just reaches out and grabs one of her hands between both of his—and asks her to run off with him in his Chevy . . . ?"

"Shoes!" Penny hissed, awakening me from my imaginings. "He's in a chair. She's on the floor—close. Their *shoes* are touching, I think."

"So old Harrington is a foot-toucher, after all," I told myself, choking back the laugh that threatened to burst from the back of my throat. I'd been right in the first place—absolutely right. I knew then that I didn't even need to be down where Penny was because I could see it all inside my head anyway. Every single thing that was going to happen in his apartment, I could see—without seeing.

But, still, I did want Penny to narrate for me—to keep feeding me news about all the tantalizing things she was actually looking at. That was what I wanted, but Penny wasn't saying a word. She was just down there, swaying slightly, squeezing her hands together, and staring into Harrington's window like she was seeing the best movie she'd ever seen in her whole life. It had drama, sex, sadness—everything, in fact, but popcorn.

"Penny . . . ," I whispered, about to ask her if she didn't wish she had a delicious box of buttered popcorn.

Her answer was brief: "Shut up." And it was said, not in the usual nice way, but looking up at me with daggers like the ones I'd seen a week ago flying through the air between her mother's eyes and her father's.

Strangely enough, however, I didn't feel like shutting up, even if it was Penny telling me to do so. "Did she bring papers—typed? You know, an envelope like last week—as her excuse?"

Penny didn't answer. She didn't even look up. Instead, as if she hadn't heard me, she just sat there unmoving, enjoying every second of what was being acted out behind the thin curtain in front of her face. She was there, all warm and happy, with her cheeks flushed rosy pink while I was left alone on the roof, cold—in her thin nylon shell—and jealous. Terribly, terribly jealous.

"Penny, Penny," I pleaded, in a tiny little voice as I began to inch forward again, farther over the edge of the fire escape. "Penny!" As I was about to plead for information and was even considering going down, without her permission, to look for myself—something awful happened.

My chest and elbows pushed a whole pile of loose gravel off the edge of the roof and sent it raining down on Penny and on the perforated metal fire escape. Clink, plink, plink, plinkety-plink was the sound the gravel made as it hit below outside Harrington's window. It may have sounded clinkety and plinkety to me, but to the two people inside Harrington's apartment it must have sounded like the beginning of a landslide.

As the gravel began to plink, Penny sprang to her feet. *She* knew what that sound was. But, although I expected her to look up at me, she didn't. For one moment she stood as if totally paralyzed, right in front of Harrington's living room window. Then, like some kind of graceful panther, she bounded down the three sets of fire escape stairs. Next she fearlessly jumped the additional eight feet to the sidewalk and, moving with breathtaking swiftness, disappeared from sight.

I would have liked to scramble along after her, but I was frozen at the edge of the roof, unable to move. I couldn't make myself run down an outside fire escape. If I did, I'd never have the courage to jump to the sidewalk. If *I* started down, I'd end up stranded there like a chicken in a wire cage.

Meanwhile, I had other—more immediate—worries. What would Martha and Harrington do now? Would they come down? How long would it take? Did they have to put their clothes back on first?

In any case, I was trapped and terrified, and I was

hating Penny. Hating her as much as I'd ever hated anybody because (and without looking up) she'd abandoned me. Just as I was beginning to allow myself to wallow in these feelings, Harrington and Martha appeared below.

There they were, already outside—both fully dressed. Martha, with a manila envelope clutched to her chest, was running off in one direction while Harrington, looking handsome and desperate, headed the other way—the way Penny had gone.

"Hey, hey . . . ," he cried in a weird, frightening croak. "Hey, hey . . . ," he repeated. "Come back! Come back, will you?" As he was calling out, he—with his long legs—bounded as Penny had done, right out of my line of vision. For a minute I could hear the faint sounds of his thudding feet and a few stray "heys," but after that I heard nothing. Nothing at all but the sound of cars whooshing by on Portola.

I was all alone on Ronald B. Harrington's roof. Then—only then—did I realize at last what Penny had really done. And she had not done it to be cruel to me but to *save* me. By showing herself clearly before she ran off, then climbing and escaping in such an open, obvious way, she had managed to protect me. Now they were all gone and I could simply open the trap door, run down the inside steps, and make a getaway without being caught. Penny had known that I'd be too afraid and too slow to keep up with her. Using a quick-witted strategy, she had risked herself—and all for me.

Now I wasn't cold or full of hate but warm, very warm. I was going to escape without danger. Then, being careful not to be seen, I'd sneak right over to Penny's apartment. There, I'd thank her for all she'd done. And later, when all that thank-you stuff was out of the way, we'd sit down together and she'd tell me, word for word, exactly what Martha and Harrington had said and every single thing they'd done.

.10.

ALTHOUGH PENNY OPENED HER FRONT DOOR PRACTICALLY before I had a chance to ring, she didn't look very happy to see me. In fact, for a second she almost glared as if I was the last person in the whole world she wanted to be looking at. Then, suddenly, her face changed. Giving me the warmest, most relieved smile, she reached out, pulled me into her apartment, and slammed the door behind us. As she was double-locking the door, she said only two words. "Thank goodness!"

". . . that it wasn't Harrington?" I asked.

"Yes," Penny agreed. "And that it's you, Pru—and that you're okay. I was *so* worried!"

While Penny and I were talking, we flopped down on the couch next to one another, but as we did, her bright-toothed smile dropped away. Using one hand to grip my elbow, she pointed with the other toward the back of the apartment.

"Mom's doing a Saturday because it's tax season," she told me soberly. "And *he's* back there—locked in the bathroom—killing himself. You can hear the shower and smell it, can't you?"

I sniffed. Yes, the smell of burning tobacco was unmistakable. "Isn't there anything you can do?" I asked, half forgetting our recent escape from Harrington's roof.

Penny twisted the gold stud in her left ear and swung her head to indicate she couldn't.

"I knocked after I got home. Knocked and banged, but he didn't answer me. Just started singing—loud—like he really was in the shower and couldn't hear me at all."

Never had I seen Penny depressed like that. She was so tense her cheeks were all pinched in, making her nose look longer than usual. Her cheeks didn't have any color in them either. They were dead white.

I knew right away that I had to do something for

her—something to take her mind completely away from her father and his dangerous, sneaky cigarette-smoking. There was, however, only one subject I could think of. It wasn't appropriate—not at all appropriate. I knew that, and yet I had to bring it up. Anything, I told my-self, that will cheer up Penny is all right—even talking about *them*.

"Harrington and Martha," I mumbled, drawing my knees up tightly next to my chest. "Did they see you?"

For a minute Penny fingered her right earlobe with-out answering. Then she shrugged. "Maybe. I suppose. Does it matter?"

"Yes, yes," I insisted. "Of course, it matters. I mean, you were there *so* long seeing what you were seeing."

As she was listening to me, Penny's face changed and she began to laugh. "That's right, Pru . . . oh, help—what I was seeing! God, with the smoke here and worrying about you, I'd almost forgotten! And—wow—what I saw!"

I'd done it. I'd snapped her out of her dark mood. "Well, come on—*tell* me," I begged, swinging my hair from side to side. "You were driving me crazy down there. You kept on sitting and sitting and not saying a word. Not a word after *feet*, you know—that he was in the chair and she was on the floor with their feet touching."

"Shoes," Penny said.

"Shoes?" I asked.

"Yes, I didn't say their feet were touching. It was their shoes. I wouldn't want to tell you anything that wasn't accurate." Penny was smiling as she talked, but she was shaking her head. "Really, you know, Pru—I shouldn't say anything. Look—it's bad enough that I was looking in. Bad enough that I saw what I saw without . . . ."

"Penny! Please, please, please," I interrupted. "You can't keep it from me. You can't! We're in this together. The two P's, remember?" As I got caught up in my "pleases," I gripped my knees even tighter.

Penny, for some reason, didn't seem to be paying any attention to my excitement. Instead, slowly and carefully, she began to unbutton the patchwork sweater. Then, taking it off and folding it, she put it down next to me. I was beginning to feel hot, angry words jumping from the top of my head down to my tongue. She wasn't going to tell me, I realized then. Not a thing. To steady myself and postpone my screams as long as possible, I began to grind my teeth together while I unwound her gauzy, coiled scarf from my head.

All of a sudden, though, Penny's mood changed again. Without warning, she began to laugh and shriek. Howling as if she was a real mental—sick, crazy, totally and absolutely mad—she rolled right off the couch onto the worn Oriental carpet. Frightened, I dropped her scarf and leaped to my feet. I was going to either run or wet my pants or both, but the sight of Penny writhing on the floor was too much. After the panic and exhaustion of spending half the day on Harrington's roof, this was more than I could handle.

I couldn't run, though, because Penny had reached out and grabbed both my ankles. Then, still choking and laughing, she was trying to tell me something.

"*Teasing*, Pru—teasing you! You're—so serious—so scared! Tell you? Of course, I'll tell you. Two P's, aren't we?"

Not three minutes later, totally under control, Penny was sitting on the floor excitedly telling me everything I wanted to know. Every single thing.

"Not just shoes," she assured me. "After a while she got up from the floor and sat in his lap, and he was touching her hair. Touching it, like it was beautiful and precious and not just Martha's nerdy, stringy stuff."

"What were they saying?" I asked.

Using both hands, Penny pushed her hair back from her face. As she did, I noticed that her cheeks were no longer pale. Mine felt fiery, too.

"What were they *saying*?"

Penny shook her head. "Nothing, I swear. Not a word. At least not one I could hear. They just kept looking, Pru. Looking and looking *passionately* into each other's eyes."

I could feel myself shivering deliciously as I pictured Martha on Harrington's lap, resting her rounded, leotarded chest against his bony, oxford-cloth-covered shoulder. While shivering, I was seeing not only Martha and him—but Anna, Hester, Rima, Jane, Scarlett, and so many others.

Before I was finished enjoying that picture, however, Penny continued speaking. "Then his hands . . . ," she said, slowly and distinctly, ". . . they moved down from her head to her neck—to the bony place, you know —the cut-out place at the top of the leotard where her bare skin shows. And . . . with just the very ends of his fingertips, Pru, the very tippy-tips, he was touching her there. . . ."

"Where?"

"At the *neck*, like I said. All around it—on the bony part. Her ears, too. And slowly . . . so slowly."

"What was *she* doing?" I whispered, matching Penny's soft voice by lowering my own.

"Nothing. Not a thing. Just sitting, sort of leaning against him, with that sappy look, you know the look.

You've seen it on her face a million times. Like when she was looking at that elephant seal baby."

My body was acting up as I listened to Penny. It was sort of twitching and quivering in a way I couldn't control. "What else? What else?" I urged as Penny failed to continue. "Did they rub their faces together? Did they hug? Did they kiss? Was it all passionate and did he touch her anywhere else? Anywhere on her body? Did he?"

"Now, don't rush me, Pru," Penny answered after a small thoughtful pause. "Don't rush because I want to tell it all slowly, the way they were moving, so you can really appreciate it. Everything, you see, they did was terribly gentle and awfully slow."

As she was speaking, she reached out and grabbed for the coiled scarf I had taken from my head. Then she wound it about herself in an entirely new and fascinating way. This time it came from behind her neck and was draped around her chest to form a cunning little striped vest.

When she began to talk again, her voice sounded entirely different. It was as grim and fierce as it had been at Ano Nuevo when she had defended Martha after Brooke called her an elephant seal. "I'm going to tell you what you want to know, Pru. Everything. But I want you to understand that what we're talking about is very serious. It's *child molesting*. After all, god, he must be almost forty and she's just twelve. But we must never tell, Pru, never tell anyone—not one single person in the world what we saw!"

She was right, of course, as usual. Scarlett, Hester, Anna, and the others faded into dusty book-jacket shadows as I thought about age twelve, age forty—and about child molesting.

While I was still brooding about this, Penny went on, slowly—slowly drawing everything out. Not only was she telling me what I wanted to know but more. Much more. It didn't seem as if she'd been down there that long watching, yet on the roof I'd lost all sense of time. As she continued telling me what Martha and Harrington had been doing together, my unreliable stomach began to act up. It was flip-flopping in a disagreeable way. Her words were making less and less sense to me, as if a thick glass window was being pulled closed between us, forcing me to look through and lip-read, instead of being able to use my ears for listening.

It was all a little fuzzy in my head, maybe because I hadn't eaten all day, but somehow while Penny was still talking, I was on my feet, holding my sweater, and backing out of her apartment. My mouth must have said something to her, explained that my stomach felt like the Maytag doing a load of dirty clothes or insisted that I ought to be getting home, yet I don't actually remember saying either of those things. My mouth was so dry, dry as if I was wandering alone in some desert (with no Maytags). Penny was there but there looking like a mirage because her teeth were wet, gleaming and without thirst in such a way that I knew she was not really where I was.

The nonexistent window was opening, though, and her voice had come back. It was very clear as it said what it had said before. "No one—absolutely no one must hear of this, Pru. You understand, don't you? A secret—an absolute and total secret, Pru. You hear me— don't you, Pru?"

I heard, all right. Not only as she said it but all the way home I heard it again as her words pounded between my ears and behind my eyes. What Penny had seen was bad, terrible, dangerous. Child molesting wasn't a private joke or something to keep secret, but something my mother, my father, and Mrs. Monzoni should know about right away. The sooner the better. Even if it got me into trouble. Even if it got Penny into trouble, too.

Promises to Penny or not, I knew as I ran that we'd send Lion out for a pound of butter and two quarts of milk, and I'd sit in Daddy's lap while he sat in his

big chair and explain to him and to Mom everything
I knew. But it didn't happen quite that way because
when I got to my front door, I found it locked. Locked
and with a note in my mother's tiny Italic writing that
said, "Gone to Marina Green to fly the kite. Come
join us, Prudie!"

If that had been all I found there, I would have
been okay, but the doorstep itself wasn't empty. Sitting
there, with slumping shoulders and brooding eyes, was
Ronald B. Harrington.

I was still squinting at my mother's note when he
started talking. "I came, Pru, because I saw you—you
at the window and running off in that crazy sweater of
yours. But where did you go? I've been waiting so long
and . . . ."

As he was talking in a horrible, half-strangled voice,
he kept pulling at his shirt collar as if it was responsible
for changing his voice. "We must talk, Pru. This is
important—very important. Do you have a key? Can
we go inside where we can talk privately?"

As soon as he said "privately," I could feel myself
getting oddly stiff. I did have a key, of course. All I
had to do was take it from the string around my neck
inside my shirt, but I wasn't going to do it. After the
things Penny had told me, I wasn't going into an
empty house alone with this handsome, nearly hysteri-

cal man, even if he did look and sound exactly like
Vronsky, Rhett, and Mr. Rochester.

"Do you have a key?" he repeated.

"No," I lied.

"Then we will just have to talk here," he told me,
frowning and motioning for me to sit on the steps next
to him. I sat, but not at all close. I sort of perched, all
the way over on the other side, holding on to the
railing.

"Now look," he said, hardly waiting for my bottom
to touch brick. "That was a damnable thing for you to
be doing, Pru—snooping like that. But you didn't see a
thing, not one single thing that I did or said or that
Martha did or said that was wrong in any conceivable
way, did you? You didn't see anything amiss, did
you?"

As I shook my head, I thought of Penny in *my*
sweater crouched outside his window while I cowered
above on the roof. "No," I said, numbly but truthfully.
"I didn't see a thing."

"Then why—why?" he began to plead, jumping to
his feet and starting to pace nervously in front of me.
"Was it your friend Penny that got you into this? I
mean . . . you do have a rather impressive imagina-
tion, Pru, but you've never been sneaky or distrustful.
It's out of character. Quite out of character for Bonnie

Phillips's daughter to be involved in an episode like this."

Suddenly he stopped pacing. Then, rubbing at his beard, he stood staring down into my face. "Look, Pru —it's as simple as this. Martha types for me. I pay her a little and also, in return, I meet with her for an hour on Saturdays to read her poems and offer critical assistance. I don't *have* to give you this explanation, you know, but there it is. Do you hear me, Pru?"

I nodded. "I hear you." I felt confused and overheated. Drops of sweat were dribbling through my thick hair and onto the back of my neck. I trusted Penny because she was my friend and she was so sincere. But this man who was looming over me—he was sincere, too.

"Poor Martha," he continued, beginning to rub his head instead of his beard. "She has little enough, living with that aunt and grandmother, without having someone start spreading malicious gossip about her. You understand that what you saw was nothing more than a rather ordinary lesson between a teacher and a pupil. You do understand, don't you?"

No, I didn't understand. I was, as I had been many times before, totally lost. The wishbone again. I was caught between Harrington's strategies (how could a Man of Mystery not have strategies?) and Penny's, and I didn't like it at all.

"You do understand?"

He stood there waiting for my answer, but no words came out of my sticky, bad-tasting mouth.

"Pru!"

"What?"

"You do understand?"

I felt hot and so shaky that when I began to nod at him, my head just kept bobbling up and down in weird, unnecessary jerks. "Yes," I said, but as I said it I knew it was just a word, a three-letter word with no meaning at all. A word spoken to get rid of him.

"Good girl," he declared with a huge sigh of relief. "The whole matter is closed. Right?"

"Right," I echoed.

Harrington smiled as I said that, a tight little smile. Then, reaching down, he touched the tip of my nose—briefly—with the end of the first finger of his left hand. As far as he was concerned, our discussion was obviously finished. Forever.

"You know what I think you should be doing, Pru? I think on a windy Saturday like this—and look, the sun has even burned through the fog—you should be out on Marina Green with your lovely mother and that nice family of yours flying a kite!"

Then, without another word, he hurried off down the block. As I watched him go, I sat on the steps picking lint balls from my sweater. Picking and thinking about

Mom, Dad, and Lion. They were down by the Bay trying to fly the homemade dragon kite while I—the true dragon—was sitting in front of our empty house feeling my fiery cheeks and wondering how long it would be before great tongues of fire started to leap out of my terrible, hot head.

Sᴜɴᴅᴀʏ ᴡᴀs ᴛʜᴇ ᴅᴀʏ I ᴄᴏᴜʟᴅɴ'ᴛ ᴇᴠᴇɴ ᴄʜᴏᴋᴇ ᴅᴏᴡɴ ᴏɴᴇ of my mother's blueberry waffles and the day I told Lion to butt out of my business and stop asking what was wrong. I couldn't talk about it. Any of it. Not until I decided who—Harrington or Penny—had lied to me.

Monday, as far as I was concerned, was only going to be the day after Sunday—a day on which I would be away from my family and back at school trying to figure out whom to believe. Things turned out to be much more complicated, however, than I could have possibly imagined. In fact, Monday, March 5th, was different from any day I'd ever spent anywhere.

I began to find this out before I even got as far as Harrington's fender. Suddenly I was surrounded by uncountable numbers of open mouths. My sixth-grade classmates and some of the younger kids, too, were yelling and pressing in close to me. Closer and closer. They made me feel like a toy boat about to be sunk by high waves on a stormy sea. Pushing me, rocking me, they kept trying to ask me something. At first none of it made any sense. Then—little by little and filled with panic—I began to hear their words.

"Harrington! Harrington and Martha!"

"Martha and him!"

"Together—doing things!"

"*Them* and at *his* flat!"

"True? Is it true?"

"Pru—about Martha and Harrington together. Tell us, Pru!"

"Tell us. Tell us!"

I know I would have just turned over and drowned with nothing but a few bubbles to show for it, but they —that sea of frantic, moving faces—were holding me up as they strained to hear my answers.

All Saturday night and Sunday I had suffered alone, trying to blot Penny's words out of my head, trying

to forget about Harrington's eyes and his totally con-
tradictory words. But it hadn't worked. I'd dragged
myself about, feeling hot and dragony, feeling like the
kind of creature that breathes fire and kills everything
it touches. If I told about Martha and Harrington, I'd
decided, I would be wrong—since I had no proof. But
if I didn't tell, I'd still be wrong. Child molesting, after
all, as Penny had said, was no kind of joke. And yet
he—Harrington—had sworn to me that nothing had
happened.

Thoroughly confused, I hadn't said a word. Not one
word to anyone—but weirdly enough, as I arrived at
school, Brooke, Alyson, and everyone already knew.

"But how?" I asked myself frantically.

Someone had told. But who? Not Harrington. Not
Martha. And certainly not . . . .

"Penny?" I gasped, trying to clear myself more space
and all. "Where's Penny?"

"Hasn't come yet," Brooke said. "No, wait—there.
There she is."

I could feel myself sighing with some small but nervous bit of relief to see Penny edging her way through
the crowd. The scarf was looped around her neck and,
with tassels swinging, she came right to my side.

"They know!" I told her, grabbing hold of her arms.
"About *them*! But how? How?" I had to shout to make

my words understandable above the other screaming voices.

Looking very concerned and important, Penny frowned. She began to give orders. "Back! Back! Get back!" As she spoke, she spun around, swinging her arms and forcing the others to step away and give us some room to breathe.

"But how do they know, Penny?" I moaned. "How?"

The answer came not from Penny but from Brooke. "Cal Williams saw you. Going there *and* on the fire escape. Now tell us, Pru. All about it. Cal told us everything you told him—later, after you'd seen them. Now—is it true? Is it?"

Listening to Brooke and remembering Cal in the park made me feel creepy all over. Sure, he'd seen me there and maybe even seen Penny in *my* sweater on Harrington's fire escape. But I hadn't talked to him about anything going on between Harrington and Martha. Not me, and now I was so mixed up, so mixed up that my stomach was lurching again.

I didn't answer Brooke. I just stood there next to Penny as if a sudden terrible paralysis had hit me, listening as the open mouths around us began shouting again. The same words—over and over—were rolling over my head.

"Pru, Pru—is it true?"

"Pru, Pru—is it true?"

"Pru, Pru—is it true?"

The first bell rang as this shouting was going on, but no one paid any attention. They just kept right on chanting.

Penny nudged me with her elbow. "You might as well tell them," she said. "Since they know already—and it is the truth. They have a right to know, don't they?"

My voice stuck somewhere down between my ribs—somewhere near where Penny had nudged me. I had expected her to order the others to bug off, yet there she was her usual, calm self, smiling as she urged me to tell. Penny was, after all, the one who had said that everything she'd seen and passed on to me had to be kept a deep, dark secret, yet now that it wasn't secret she didn't seem to be the least bit upset. Instead, her eyes were sparkling as she looked at the faces around us.

"Tell them, Pru. Go on," she coaxed.

"Can't," I mumbled, trying to swallow down my breakfast of Rice Krispies, which seemed to be snap-crackle-and-popping its way to the back of my throat. "Not now—can't now. . . ."

The second bell was ringing and Mrs. Monzoni, looking wildly upset, was in the yard with a megaphone, sending threats in every direction. This morning she didn't look like any French pastry but like a yellow-haired, red-faced wooden marionette, held together by string and Scotch tape. She jerked and moved about with odd, twitching steps as she shrieked through the megaphone. "Homerooms or else!" she was saying. "Homerooms! Homerooms! Homerooms—or else!"

With a general groan my curious, excited classmates stopped chanting and began, with grumbling disappointment, to do as they had been ordered.

"Later," Penny told everyone encouragingly. "Later—at lunch or recess. Ask her later."

Then, to hurry them up, she reminded Brooke and some others from our homeroom that they were about to go into #307 where they would have a special treat. They'd be able to stare at Harrington and Martha, *together*. And that did it. With enthusiasm, they all began to press from the yard into the red brick school building.

"Don't hurry," Penny said, tugging at my sweater. "I have to tell you something."

"What?" I asked, hoping she'd tell me how Cal Williams knew what he knew. What she said, however, left me even more confused and upset.

"You've got to pull yourself together, Pru. Handle

yourself better. Don't you see—you're a heroine now. A real, genuine, Portola Hill heroine. A leader-type! Not a nerd. Not a nobody, but important—a *real somebody*. But you must be brave and speak up and tell them exactly what you saw. Now you're a leader and everybody knows it! So you must tell every little thing."

I could feel myself shuddering as I listened to Penny. I was being encouraged to be a leader-heroine by telling about things I'd never seen. I was being urged to be a despicable liar. All *I'd* ever seen was someone who looked like me—my hair and my sweater—peeking into someone else's window.

"What if . . . ?" I asked myself as I followed Penny up the steps toward Harrington's homeroom. "What if . . . what if. . . what if . . . ?" But like a warped record, my thoughts wouldn't finish. The only thing in my head, as I forced myself to continue to that room where I'd have to see a pair of deep-set eyes digging into me, was "What if . . . what if . . . ?"

I didn't have to see those eyes, however, because Harrington wasn't there. A round-faced, solid-looking woman, who pounded for silence with *his* yardstick, introduced herself as Mrs. Dina Sack and told us to take our seats. Immediately! I felt a tiny twinge of relief when I knew I wasn't going to have to face Harrington.

When I glanced around the classroom as Penny and I slid into our seats, I suddenly realized something else. Martha Brandeberry wasn't there, either. That didn't make me feel better, though. Quite the opposite. It unlocked all the dreadful what-ifs that had been stuttering around inside my head.

"What if . . . Harrington and Martha have run off together? What if . . . he's been arrested for child molesting and she's been put in a mental ward? What if . . . they've decided to—to commit suicide? That the only way out is suicide . . . ?"

"Step outside," a voice by my left ear was saying. It appeared to be floating out of the mouth of that round-faced Mrs. Sack. "Pru Phillips—that's you, isn't it? Step outside."

". . . suicide," I mumbled.

"Yes," she answered brusquely. "That's right—outside and down to Mrs. Monzoni's office. Now."

As I rose to my feet, Penny tried to give me a sympathetic little pat on my right arm, but instead of looking down at her—hoping to pick up some of her courage—I just shook off her hand and headed up the aisle. Then, conscious of nothing but my tumbly stomach, I walked out of #307, down the stairs, and across the hall to Mrs. Monzoni's office.

Without a word, the secretary twitching his mustache in a grim, peculiar way motioned me to proceed into the inner office. I'd never been in there before— not once in my year and a half at Portola Hill. My feet in Penny's clogs, obedient to Mrs. Sack's orders, kept plunking themselves one in front of the other until they had moved the rest of me into the office, near a large oak desk scattered with papers.

After the desk, the walls were the first thing I noticed —chewing-gum brown, with the picture of George Washington (his mouth held stiff over wooden teeth) that every school I've ever been in has had. After that, I saw the blossoms. Sprigs of fresh, pink plum blossoms in a vase on one corner of the desk. They were so tender, so delicate and romantic, somehow, like something out of *The Scarlet Letter* that they made me feel like crying.

Only then did I see the people. Predictable again, entirely predictable. Martha and Harrington, who had *not* run off or committed suicide, sitting on opposite sides of the office. Her eyes were examining the wooden floor planks, circling the toes of her ballet slippers but always fastened on the floor. His eyes were not on the floor. They were boring into me, and he was mumbling something about the Ides of March. Mrs. Monzoni was there, of course. So were Martha's aunt and grandmother, sober, silent, and staring va-

cantly across the office. Both of them wore crinkly
cotton dresses with flowers and had their hair pulled
back, stringy hair a little grayer but otherwise not
much different from Martha's. Their faces reminded
me of a painting of a woman I'd seen once (in one of
those places we'd lived) called *American Gothic*. If I
had what-iffed this scene, I would have done it exactly
that way. Only one thing was missing. My mother and
my father. But Mrs. Monzoni was already explaining
about that.

". . . haven't called them yet, Prudence, because we
felt you should have a chance to explain yourself."

That made sense. Mrs. Monzoni, I realized suddenly,
was not just a pretty piece of pastry. That had been
a silly student joke. She was a serious, hard-working
woman with a school full of dreadful students like me
that created a never-ending riot of problems. And,
thank goodness, she was willing to believe me inno-
cent until I was proven to be guilty.

"Prudence," she said again. "Pru? Are you listening
to me?"

"Yes," I answered. "I'm sorry. . . ."

"Then sit down—yes, in that chair there—and tell me
just what you think has been going on."

"Can I stand?" I asked softly, knowing that sitting
was going to put disagreeable pressure on my stomach.

She nodded. "All right. Of course—if you wish. Now, concerning these outrageous rumors, which seem to have turned the sixth grade and half the others into a hysterical mob—what would you like to tell us?"

"Nothing," I said truthfully, wanting to glance sideways and catch a glimpse of Harrington. I didn't do it, though, because I was afraid I'd crumple to the floor, mortally wounded, if I allowed his eyes to shoot through me again.

"About Mr. Harrington and Martha," my principal prompted with a firm but not unkind manner. "Were you there Saturday—at his flat?"

Reluctantly, I nodded. "Yes."

"Speak up, I can't hear you."

"Yes," I repeated numbly. I wasn't lying. Yes, I had been there. I just hadn't been looking in the window. Nor had I spread any stories.

"Prudence—these are very serious charges you've made—the things you've been so free about telling the other students. Martha says she was delivering typed papers. Mr. Harrington says he was taking back his papers and helping her with her poetry. Is that what you saw? Or did you see something else?"

"I didn't see anything," I answered, knowing then and there that even to protect myself . . . or Penny—I wasn't going to tell any lies. Whatever I said in this office, it would at least be truthful.

Although no one had encouraged Martha to speak up, quite suddenly she did. "I took him his papers and mine," she said, looking for all the world as if she were reading the words right off the floor boards. "He said . . . would I like coffee and that I was using too many adjectives and I reminded him that I didn't like coffee but that I liked adjectives."

Martha's words were sad, pathetic, and nerdy, but they were funny, too. Funny like her brilliant observation (while apologizing for the skipping *A*'s on her aunt's typewriter) about how many words had *A*'s in them. For some strange reason, I wanted to laugh—shriek and howl with laughter as Penny had laughed at me on Saturday. But I didn't, because when I thought of Penny, I felt all sober again.

Penny, Penny. She was part of this drama, too. "Where is Penny?" I began to ask myself. "Why isn't she here with me?"

We were, after all, the two P's. Two P's in a pod. And what a pod it was! She should be standing at my side, sharing the responsibility for this sickening mess. But she wasn't. I wouldn't have let *her* go to Mrs. Monzoni's office alone, I told myself. Or would I? And how had Cal Williams known those things if she . . . ?

Mr. Harrington was speaking now. His voice, deep and thundery with emotion, broke into my thoughts.

"This is very serious. Desperately important. You didn't see *anything—anything not right,* did you, Pru?"

"No," I said, staring forward at the plum blossoms instead of sideways toward his face.

"So why . . . ," he continued, his voice still rumbling, ". . . why did you tell such damnable . . . no, no— wait!" He paused for a very long, miserable minute and took a deep breath. Then, using an entirely different approach, he spoke again. "What about *Penny Hoffman?* Let's go back to Penny. Where was she on Saturday? Was she with you? Is she involved in this mess? Is she? Is she?"

I just stood there as he talked, lowering my eyes from the blossoms to the blue glass vase. Azure blue glass with bubbles in it. Bubbles trapped in glass like the bubbles in my stomach.

"I can't believe, Pru, that you—alone—would do something as despicable as this. People's whole lives can be ruined—tragically—by lies like these. Look, you've been a nice, responsible girl since you came here last year. You've never before been in any kind of trouble. So tell me—tell us all—if Penny was there, too."

Again, instead of answering, I concentrated on the blue glass vase.

"Prudence, Mr. Harrington is asking you something, and I insist upon an answer from you."

I nodded obediently at Mrs. Monzoni. Then, very slowly, I let my feet turn my body until it was facing *him* where he sat, crunching his knuckles together.

"Pru," he said simply, holding my eyes with his. "Answer. About Penny . . . answer. . . ."

Penny. Penny. Penny. Strategy. Strategy. Penny and I—we were the two P's. Two P's in a pod. Well, I didn't like the pod we were in. Not any more. I wanted out! But I wasn't a fink. I had never been a fink. . . .

"About Penny . . . ," Harrington repeated, his voice beginning to crack.

As if I was about to reply to his words, I opened my mouth—a little at first, then wider and wider. No words came out, though. Instead, leaning forward, I vomited. Pea-green vomit, all over Mrs. Monzoni's wood-planked office floor. Over the floor and over Penny's blue clogs, which were squeezing my toes.

.12.

They sent me home. It wasn't a punishment, really. At least not completely. The corners of Mrs. Monzoni's eyes wrinkled up with what looked like concern (instead of disgust) as she herself hustled me down to the girls' bathroom to help me clean myself up a little before I left.

When I saw all the horrible, many-colored "loves" crawling all over the bathroom walls, I almost vomited again. But by sort of half closing my eyes, I managed to control myself during the two or three minutes I had

to spend in there. Mrs. Monzoni was helpful with hand-
fuls of wet, rough washroom towels and, thank goodness, she was also silent. She didn't say anything to me,
so I didn't have to say anything to her. Then, as soon
as I had finished wiping my face and Penny's clogs, I
left Portola Hill and headed straight for my own house.

What I was going to say or do when I got there was
bothering me, but I needn't have worried because no
one was home. Taking the key from around my neck,
I let myself into the house, where I found the living
room and kitchen empty of people but full of things
that reminded me of each member of my family. The
family I'd paid so little attention to since Penny and I
had become friends.

Instead of heading right for the bathroom and trying
to wash all the sick off me in the shower, I just stood
there for the longest time, looking around but not touching anything. I saw my books, my latest stack of library
books—*Wuthering Heights, Love Story, Pride and Prej-
udice, Daddy Long-Legs*. I also saw eggs, painted and
half painted. And brushes scattered next to jars of
luscious-colored acrylics. A typewriter with reference
books about fish piled up next to it. In the typewriter
was a sheet of paper with only a few lines of print . . .
a paper simply left floating there when my mom ran
out of words. . . .

Lion's latest jigsaw was there, too, and a new junk sculpture he'd been working on. Glued down to the board this time were a lot of things I'd given him during Christmas vacation when I cleaned my closet. I could see a Barbie doll in a strapless dress, her arms spread straight out to the sides (Ruthie and I used to play Barbies together), some jacks, an old birthday party hat and some plastic beads, a little china mouse with one foot missing, a jump-rope handle, plastic cups and saucers from a tiny tea set I'd had, and several disgusting pieces of leftover Halloween candy. A lot of other junk, in between these things, also reminded me of when I'd been younger. Too young to worry about having the *right* best friend and about being popular. Too young to read romantic books. Too young to spy and ruin people's lives.

Tears had started dribbling out of my eyes. They were blurring all the stuff on Lion's sculpture. He would blur it anyway when he spray-painted over it, turning all the items into shadowy white outlines. Looking through tears at those things reminded me so much of Ruthie that, for a moment, I thought I'd rush right back to my room and write her to tell her about Martha, Harrington, Penny, and the horrible mess I'd gotten myself into. But wiping at my tears with the cuff of my shirt, I already knew I wouldn't do it. We'd stopped exchanging letters more than eight months ago.

It took me a very long time, but finally I stopped thinking about Ruthie and staring down at the old junk glued onto Lion's sculpture. When I did, my father's chair caught my eye. There it was, surrounded, as usual, by an untidy assortment of archaeological books on Crete, Guatemala, and Cambodia as well as over-full folders of Xeroxed smog papers. Looking at this familiar scene, I suddenly remembered some words my father had said days and days ago.

Giving in to a sudden impulse, I scrunched myself up in the old chair, which was hollowed out to fit his large shape, and pretended he was there between me and the saggy plaid fabric. Not only was he there, but he was saying those words all over again. "I have a feeling that with Penny you're only as good as your last deal. . . ."

Though I'd never questioned him about the exact meaning of that sentence, this terrible morning it was beginning to come to me all on my own. Penny. Penny. Strategy. Strategy. Penny was supposed to be my best friend. At least, I had called her that. But how had it happened? How had Penny attached herself to a nerd like me?

Slowly—ever so slowly—it was beginning to be clear enough for me to understand. Penny was my friend, not because we looked alike and not because she really cared about me, but because I had always done just about *every single thing she had ever asked me to.* And without a single yell. I knew now that I had made a mistake by not yelling or pinching hard enough when she sat down next to me on Harrington's fender and simply *told* me she was a leader. Instead I had believed her. Then, having me there looking alike and so obedient had been useful—for her strategies. To her—it was true—I was only as good, as Daddy had so cruelly told me, as my last deal. "What if . . . ?" I asked myself. "What if . . . I didn't do as she said? Hadn't done as she said? What if . . . what if . . . ?"

As I was suffering over these thoughts, I found myself reaching up to my left earlobe. But instead of fingering the smooth gold stud as Penny and I had gotten into the habit of doing, I reached around to the back of my ear and touched the little screw-in thing. It was larger than the stud and flat, with rough, fluty little edges. A thin, sharp piece—called the *post,* I think—stuck out in the middle. For a minute or two I just kept on using my fingers to explore the size and shape of the post and its fluted disc. Then, without really thinking about what I was doing, I began to tighten my fingers and yank at the disc. Its rough edge fitted right under my fingernails. Taking a good, firm grip on it, I began to pull. I pulled and kept on pulling. Pulling and twisting and paying no attention to the horrible, tearing pain.

I kept struggling and twisting until, with one final, desperate tug, the disc twisted loose from the post. Then, reaching forward, I jerked the gold stud from my ear and flung it down on the floor. I didn't see it, but I could hear the clink as it bounced against Lion's sculpture. Next, without pausing for the teeniest minute, I used my fingernails to dig under the disc behind my right ear. Gripping hold of it, I worked until I twisted that one loose, too, so I could take the other stud and send it skidding across the floor to its look-alike.

My ears were both oozy and full of throbbing pain. But I didn't move. I just sat there in Daddy's chair, letting loose all the what-ifs I'd never dared to think, much less *say*. "What if . . . Penny really hates me? What if . . . she has always hated me and has thought all along I was just a nerd like Martha? What if . . . she lied—lied and lied—about what she said she saw in Harrington's flat? What if . . . what . . . ?"

". . . are you doing home?" Mom was asking me, shaking me out of a deep, black sleep. As she knelt in front of me reaching out, she was sniffing. She could smell the vomit and knew, in her own parent-y way, that the rotten smell came from inside me as well as out. My ears, too. She was seeing how mutilated they were as she reached up and gently touched them. "Oh, Pru . . . Pru, my girl. What is it? What's happened? What? Penny—is it Penny?"

Slowly—very slowly—I nodded. But as I did, I was grinding my teeth together to maintain self-control. This time, I was promising myself, I was not going to cry.

"Oh, Pru—look at you. Oh, come, come now, you must tell me, sweets, talk to me. I'm sorry I wasn't here when you came—been selling some of my eggs down at Taylor and Ng's. But I'm here now. Pru—I'm here. What is it?"

"I can't talk about it," I told her.

"What do you mean, you can't talk about it? Of course, you can. Oh, please, Prudie—you're all tied up in knots, and we ought to know why!"

"No," I said, feeling both tight and stubborn at the same time. "I'm not going to tell. Not going to talk. Just not going to. Do you hear me? It's my business. Mine. I'm not going to talk about it now—and you can't make me!"

I was beginning to yell and Mom, listening to me, was beginning to get very emotional, too. "Pru, Pru . . . ," she pleaded. "Look at me. I'm here. I'm your mother. I love you. When something's wrong—anything—you should be able to talk to me. Anytime, about anything! Look at me. Stop staring over my shoulder and look at me, will you?"

Against all my better instincts, I did as she asked and looked at her. Then I wished I hadn't because her unhappy face made me want to open my mouth and spill out a river of words—a fast-running river of thousands of words to tell her about Martha and Harrington . . . and about Penny, too. But I didn't. There would be time for all that later—when Daddy was here. When I was calmer.

I did say something. What I said, though, was kind of strange. It had a little bit to do with Penny. But not just with Penny. . . .

"Who is your best friend, Mommy? Do you have a best friend?"

"What?" she said, rocking back on her heels. "What?"

"I said—who is your best friend?"

Running her hands through her short, curly hair, she took a couple of minutes to think about what I'd asked. Then, laughing nervously, she shrugged her shoulders. "But I don't have *a* best friend. Well—look—what I mean is . . . that I have several. When I was younger, friends and best friends were something I thought about a lot. They were awfully important. . . ."

"But what about *now*?"

"Now? Well now, Prudie, I have you and Daddy. And Lion, of course. All three of you. It may sound a little crazy, and yet now my best friends seem to be you—my family. But why are you asking that? What does it have to do with Penny and with your poor messed-up ears?"

"I don't know," I admitted as I reached up and touched the crusty, clotted wound on my left lobe. "I'm not sure. I have to figure it all out, and I will, and when I do—then I'll tell you and Daddy and Lion. Everything. I promise. Everything. . . ."

I meant what I was telling her, but everything did have to wait. I had fallen asleep, slept half the day, maybe, in my father's chair, but now that I was awake, I still smelled bad. I still hurt, inside and out. My problem wasn't a dreaming nightmare. It was a wide-awake daymare. Something that I had to solve by myself. About Penny and Harrington and Martha. Not until I worked things out would the hurt and smell go away.

"But your ears, Pru," Mom pleaded. "Why in the world did you just rip those things out? What possessed you to do that, and don't you think Dr. Kerwin should see them?"

"No," I told her, noticing suddenly that Lion was home, too. He was lurking behind the kitchen doorway, snooping, but giving himself away because a few wild curls and the rounded edge of his stomach were visible. "It's all right, Mom, really. I just decided I didn't want them any more. That's all."

As soon as I said this, Lion showed himself, shaking his head and grinning. "Can I have them then? Can I? I need something just like that to finish my sculpture. I'll spray the paint first. Then I'll glue them on all shiny right in the middle. In Barbie's hands maybe. . . . Can I have them, Pru? Huh?"

"But, Prudie," Mom insisted, "I really think we should see Kerwin and . . . ."

"No," I interrupted. "No! No! They'll be all right. And Lion—yes, yes—you can have the studs. I don't want them."

"Are you sure?" he asked suspiciously.

"Sure I'm sure."

Hardly waiting for my answer, Lion scrambled across the floor and grabbed them as if they were some kind of precious treasure. Then, squinting to see me between loops of his hair, he said, "So you've had it with Penny, huh?"

"I don't want to talk about it," I told him, trying to remember that he was only nine and quite a bit less understanding and tactful than Mom.

"Oh, yes, Pru—you've had a big fight and you're never going to speak to her again," he rushed on. "And I told you. Remember? I told you the very first day I ever saw her. Remember—she said that if I was a lion I should roar, and I told her I was a scratching lion and that I didn't like . . . ."

"Shut up!" I yelled, using my meanest, non-Penny-sounding voice and pressing my hands tightly against my terribly tender, wounded ears. "Shut up, Shut up! Shut up!"

.13.

By covering my ears and running out of the room, I could escape from Lion's voice, but there didn't seem to be any way to shut off the voice inside my head. It kept reminding me I had important things to settle. Things with Penny, with Martha, and with Harrington. Nothing in my whole life was right, and nothing was ever going to be right until I figured out what to do.

My figuring was postponed, though, by my anxious

mother. Therefore, I didn't escape the visit to Dr. Kerwin's office (he gave us samples of some antibiotic ointment and told Mom I'd survive); nor—when we got back home—did I escape from my father.

Before he would leave me alone in my room where I wanted to be, he planted himself in my doorway and insisted that we have a few words together. But "together" wasn't really the right word for it, since almost all the words were his. They were words about Penny.

"There's something wrong with that girl," he kept telling me, repeating himself and using seven or eight different ways to say the same thing. (As if I didn't know it by now anyway. . . .) "I don't like what she's done to you, Pru—or what she's doing to you. And I think you'd better come up with some way to handle things before your mom and I feel we have to step in and do something. Do you understand me?"

"Yes," I told him. Of course, I understood. Loud and clear. "Yes . . . yes, but Daddy—for now, please—let me think. Let me work it out. By myself. Me—alone. . . ."

"All right," he agreed. "All right. Go to it—and good luck. But if you need me or any of us—we're always here, you know."

With these words, he left me right where I had said

I wanted to be. In my room where I could do some serious thinking. Except to shower and get rid of the sick smell, I didn't come out—not even for dinner. Not even when Penny called—and she must have rung our number a dozen times. But I refused to go and talk to her. I kept telling Mom, through the closed door, to tell her I was *too busy*. And I was.

Too busy even to go to sleep, so—I sat there all night staring blindly into the blackness, waiting and pressing Kleenexes against my aching ears. Then when the Tuesday A.M. sky was beginning to show its soft, pale, grayish-pink morning look, I suddenly knew what I should do.

Filled from head to toe with unusual courage and cunning, I would dress, eat, brush my teeth, and take myself—in Penny's clogs—back to Portola Hill. Even though I hadn't figured out what to do about Harrington or Martha, I did know what to do about her. I knew how to handle things. How to make them different.

To my surprise, though, when I got to school, everything was already different. Starting with Harrington's '58 Chevy. Instead of being parked in its usual spot next to the yard, it was across the street in the driveway of his building. Mr. Harrington, everyone told me, was taking "a temporary leave of absence." That was the big news buzzing through the yard as I arrived.

Other things were changed, too, as I quickly discovered. All the bathrooms had signs posted saying FRESH PAINT. Every single name and all the "loves" had been wiped out overnight by thick, glossy layers of white paint. Paint so blindingly white and forbidding, so incredibly pure that no one would dare mess it up with a felt pen. Well . . . not quite yet.

Mrs. Sack was going to sit at Harrington's desk, use his yardstick to rule over Homeroom #307, and teach his English classes as a "long-term permanent substitute"—whatever that meant. Also, according to Cal Williams, Martha was gone. She was being sent to San Mateo, to stay with her horsey, unloving mother. Being sent to a new school where she would be *their* sixth-grade class nerd.

And then, last but certainly not least—there was Penny. She, too, had changed. Her long black hair was gone. Instead, her hair was cut short—cut in such a way that her head was covered by soft, wavy curls. She was wearing a white T-shirt just tight enough to show the tips of her just-beginning-to-develop breasts, and a white denim wraparound skirt. "I've never ever seen her in a skirt before," I was telling myself as I noticed her ears.

Even they were different. Despite the fact that it

hadn't been a month since Ear-Piercing Saturday, she, too, had removed the tiny gold studs. Only instead of ripping at her earlobes she had simply unscrewed the studs and replaced them with delicate earrings made of iridescent blue-green feathers. In short, she not only looked different, but she looked *chic*—so unbelievably chic that I knew, as soon as I saw her, that she was already deep into some new strategy.

I didn't care, though. Because I was different, too. For once, *I* had my own strategy. And a good one— even if it had taken me a whole, depressing, sleepless night to come up with it. For my strategy, I didn't have to look chic—only simple but slightly mysterious. To achieve this look, I was wearing my usual pair of jeans, a shirt (not buttoned backward), a pair of pink-lensed sunglasses borrowed from my mother, and an old red-and-black cotton bandanna. The bandanna was tied around my head to hide my crusty, oozing earlobes.

When Penny bounced up next to me, shaking her short curls and smoothing her skirt, I didn't say anything about the way she looked. Even when she fingered her feathered earlobes as she was pushing me into the freshly painted yard bathroom where we could talk alone, I didn't make any comments.

What I did do—as soon as we were inside the bathroom—was slide her clogs off my feet. "These are too tight," I told her. "Can I have my Keds back?"

"Sure," she agreed, using the toes of the tennis shoes to push them off her feet without bothering to untie them. Her eyes and teeth were shining as usual, but for once—without even having to strain to resist her spell— I didn't find that look very wonderful. "Sure, here . . . ," she said as she kicked the shoes toward me with her bare toes. "The clogs will go better with my skirt anyway."

Still not allowing myself to mention her skirt, her earrings, or her haircut, I bent down and with great care began to loosen the knots in my shoelaces.

"Hey, Pru," Penny said. "You haven't even said hi this morning and you wouldn't talk last night. What's up?"

I didn't answer her. Instead, I slipped my feet into my comfortable (although slightly too warm from Penny's hot toes) Keds and tied them in double bows. Then, standing up, I started to walk out of the bathroom.

"Pru? What's wrong? Why won't you talk? And why do you look so weird today? Those sunglasses—god— and that red snotrag tied around your head . . . ."

As she kept talking, I kept walking.

"Pru! Pru! Stop!"

At last, right in the open doorway, I paused and turned back to look at her. "Why?"

"Because . . . because I want to know what's wrong."

"Nothing," I told her, shifting my weight as though I was going to leave.

"Come on, Pru," she said, almost begging. "Don't leave. What's going on? You can't leave yet. You have to tell me what happened yesterday in Monzoni's office. And listen—I've promised Brooke and some of the others you'll tell them today about Martha and Harrington. You know—about their feet touching and her on his knees and him touching her neck and . . . ."

"Shut up," I yelled, making sure my voice was good and loud.

"What?" she asked, totally shocked both by my words and by my tone of voice.

"I said—*shut up!*" I repeated, staring with my green eyes into hers. Hers may have been shining, but mine —I knew—were sending angry sparks out in her direction.

As I continued to yell, telling her over and over again to shut up, she lunged forward, grabbing me by the elbows so that our faces were very close together. "Cool it. Don't blow it," she urged in that pretty pink-cheeked way of hers. Her urging had to be very loud, too, to be heard over my yelling. "*You* are now *the* most important person in the whole sixth grade—and you mustn't blow it, Pru."

"Why not?" I asked hotly.

"Because . . . because I made everybody wait yesterday after you went home—for *you* to come back and tell everything."

"So what?"

"Pru Phillips—what's wrong with you? Aren't we the two P's? Hey—wait a minute. Wait . . . wait— you didn't tell yesterday, did you? Tell I was there? You didn't. No, you couldn't have because they didn't come for me. They would have come for me, too, if . . . . Did you tell? Did you?" she demanded, beginning to shake me angrily.

"Shut up and let go of me," I shouted. "If you want to know what happened in Mrs. Monzoni's office, why don't you walk right in and ask? Or sneak up under her window and see what you can find out that way?"

"Pru!"

"Shut up!" I insisted. "It's my turn to talk. I don't feel like listening to you. Or like being popular and being a leader—unless *I* want to be and not because you tell me that's what I'm going to be. Or because you tell me how to act, how to dress, what to say, and when to say it!" The words were spilling out of my mouth fast and fiery now. All the arguments I'd *not* had with Penny I was having right here, now. All of them at once. The volcano inside me had begun to erupt and there would be no stopping it now.

"If I want to talk to you, walk with you, sit with you," I raged on breathlessly, "I'll do it. And if I don't, I won't. So stop giving me that wet, slimy smile of yours. Stop bossing me around. If I want to be a nerd—and wear a snotrag, as you called it—around my head, I will. If I don't, I won't. And—listen—I'm just one P— *me—Pru*! If I want to be with you, I will, and if I don't, I won't. Right now—for instance—I don't. So bug off, will you?"

By now she was staring at me in a state of total shock.

Before she could recover any of her usual smooth-talking manner, I gave her the freezing-flesh-to-stone glare I usually reserved for Lion. "Go away! Leave me alone!"

"Pru?" she said, backing up a few steps and twisting her hands together in front of her chic white skirt. "Are you sick? You're acting weird. You never yell. Not you. But now—you sound like a mental. Look— look out there, see. . . . They're all waiting for us, I mean for *you*, to tell. . . ."

As she was speaking, I looked out into the yard. There was no pressing sea of faces this morning, just little ripples of movement where small groups of students stood, whispering and pointing toward where we were standing arguing in the doorway of the bathroom.

"Then *I'll* tell," I told Penny, my voice suddenly quiet again. "But by myself. I don't need you there stepping on my toes. Since *I* was on the fire escape looking in, I'll tell. But I'll tell without your help. Now get lost, will you?"

Leaving her there with her mouth hanging open, I strode into the yard, heading straight for Brooke and Alyson.

"What happened in Monzoni's office?" Alyson whispered. "And what were Martha and Harrington really doing when you saw them?"

Moving in so my head was right next to their pairs of matching ladybug earrings, I began whispering to A & B. What I whispered was quiet and brief. "I didn't see anything. Didn't see Martha *or* Harrington together —so I can't tell you about *them*! But I can tell you what happened in Mrs. Monzoni's office. . . ."

"Oh, goodie!" Brooke croaked. "What? What?"

"Well, I went in there," I began, drawing every syllable out very slowly, "and . . . they all talked and asked me a lot of questions and there were fresh plum blossoms on her desk and . . . ."

"And? And?" Alyson coaxed, leaning in so close we bumped heads.

"And then," I told them, still whispering, ". . . then —I vomited all over the floor!"

The minute I said vomit both Alyson and Brooke began to double up with laughter. "That's it? That's all?" they finally managed to ask between giggly laughs.

"Right!" I said. "But—don't tell anyone. It's a secret."

That got everything started. From then on until the second bell rang, during breaks between class and in morning recess, I continued my whisper strategy, refusing to speak to more than two or three people at a time. Telling them nothing more than I had told Brooke or Alyson—then swearing them, too, to secrecy.

For that morning—that one morning—I had a real taste of popularity. Everyone wanted to see me, whisper with me. It was a strange and exciting feeling to know that I was suddenly more important than anyone at Portola Hill. It was exciting, though, sort of in the way it would be if I was on a stage playing a part that really wasn't me. A long play because it kept going on and on. Everywhere I turned I had friends (at least temporary ones) and an audience. Part of my audience was whispering eagerly with me. But the most im-

portant member of that audience—Penny Hoffman—
was just watching.

Everywhere I whispered, she was nearby watching.
She just stood there, dressed in white, fingering her
earrings and making no attempt to rush around to
others to see what I was whispering about. Her eyes
glittered and her cheeks were more flushed than ever
as she hung back, wildly jealous that I and I alone appeared to be taking full credit for being brave enough
to climb onto Harrington's fire escape to spy on his
personal life.

After a while, my voice began to get hoarse from all
those stage whispers, and I found—to my surprise—that
the whole scene was turning into a total bore. Besides,
there were beginning to be rumblings from some students who were not at all impressed by vomit and who
were demanding to know why I was *lying* instead of
telling about what I'd seen. Ronald B. Harrington had,
after all, been a very popular—if mysterious—teacher at
Portola Hill. Now he was gone and Mrs. Sack, who
looked like one, would hardly add any excitement to
their days.

Everything was perfect, though, as far as I was concerned, because Penny was being completely, absolutely totally ignored.

By lunchtime, I knew, she'd spring into action. By

then she'd have a new, old strategy all ready to go. *The Confession Strategy.* I'd seen her confess before —seen it with Brooke and Alyson, seen it in my own kitchen when she'd confessed to breaking my mother's precious egg. I knew she would do it. And do it well. She could and she would. At lunchtime, it would happen. And I could, with no effort in the least, what-if it all. . . .

.14.

I WAS RIGHT, TOO. BY LUNCHTIME PENNY WAS A WHITE
whirlwind, spinning through the yard, telling everyone loudly and boldly that *she* in my sweater had been
the brave person spying on that fire escape. That *she*
in her clever, clever way had fooled *me* into thinking
she'd seen romantic things going on between Martha
and Harrington. She—Penny—had seen everything.

And, she confessed, everything was NOTHING.
Nothing but those two looking over typed sheets of
paper and discussing adjectives and the fact that

Martha used too many of them. Nothing was going on between Martha and Harrington. Nothing at all—except that Martha, poor nerdy Martha, probably had a silly crush on him. Even if he didn't care about her one little bit.

Penny, the True Leader and Superstar, with her smiles and bright eyes, was hypnotizing the whole school as she gave her passionate, truthful confession. Those new feathered earrings seemed to carry her off the ground as she flew from group to group explaining how sly she'd been and how stupid I'd been to believe her. Penny. Penny. Penny. All she failed to confess was that *she*—not I—had been responsible for talking with Cal and spreading the rumors.

Strangely enough, though, I didn't even care. I sat in the corner of the yard, peacefully quiet for the first time in days, chomping on carrot sticks and a peanut-butter and bacon sandwich. I felt very, very relieved to be free of the need to tell secrets of any kind. My strategy was finished. The sixth graders—well, they could hate me or laugh at me if they wanted. One morning of popularity had been much too exhausting. Anyway, now they had Penny. I had, of my own free will, given Penny to them. They could love her or turn against her if or when they found out how rotten she was inside. (They could find out the hard way, as I had, that with her you were only as good as your last deal.) But, still, I wasn't really happy because in some strange way I couldn't help worrying about Penny. About what was wrong with her. About what was going to become of someone like that. . . .

And that was exactly what I was worrying about when, suddenly, I caught sight of Martha. Chaperoned by her grandmother, she was coming out of the yard door. Her arms were full of papers, which obviously had just been cleaned out of her old desk and locker. Seeing Martha, who, like Penny, still needed worrying about, brought the dull, thumping pain back into the bottom of my stomach. Because of what *I'd* done with Penny, she was being sent back to live with her mother again. A mother who seemed, everyone said, to love horses more than her own daughter. And it was my fault. All my fault for not standing up to Penny.

Before I knew quite what I was doing, I found myself jumping up from the splintery bench and rushing over toward Martha and her grandmother.

"Martha," I gasped, feeling panicky as I waited for my brain to start telling my tongue what it was supposed to say. It didn't.

"Martha . . . Martha . . . ," I found myself repeating as I nervously tightened the bandanna wrapped around my still-throbbing ears.

Martha stared right past me as if I wasn't even there. (Nerd Pride, I guess.) Her grandmother, however, was not quite so self-controlled. With a bruising, steel-fingered grip, she grabbed at my arm. "Get away, you nasty little troublemaker," she said threateningly. "Get away before I pick you up and shake you 'til your teeth rattle!"

Startled, I backed up a few steps, but I didn't give up. I still felt I had things I must say to Martha. The words had dribbled down. They were on my tongue now all ready to spill out, so—grandmother or no grandmother—I started right in. "Martha . . . listen . . . you must listen. I'm sorry! So sorry for everything that happened. Look—I feel awful. Oh, Martha . . . I am so sorry!"

I went on and on that way, pouring out the stupid, meaningless words in a way that disgusted me because, somehow, I could hear myself sounding like Penny Hoffman. And still, I went on. ". . . oh, please listen. Please—don't just . . . ."

But she didn't listen. She and her grandmother just kept walking, forcing me to keep backing up. They were leaving, walking right out of the schoolyard, and I hadn't managed to say a single word to ease the pain in my stomach. I would never see Martha again. Never have a chance to make up for the terrible things I'd done. Never.

"Wait, Martha . . . wait," I pleaded, gripping the chain link fence. "Wait . . . oh, please wait!"

"No," Martha said, "no, no . . ." There were tears trickling out of the corners of her eyes as she spoke. "Go away," she told me.

"But, Martha . . . ."

"Go away, Prudence. Nothing you say makes any difference. I hate you all! Loathe you. Mr. Harrington—he says I have qualities that will be greatly appreciated as I grow older. Qualities that will be highly prized. But I wonder because now nobody . . . nobody . . . gives a damn about me!"

"But, Martha . . . ," I repeated, still clutching at the rusty fence and wishing I didn't sound so much like a warped record.

Martha wasn't about to listen to me, though. By now she was sobbing, with her stringy dishwater hair hanging so far forward over her books and papers that I couldn't even see her face. "Shut up," she pleaded between hiccupping gasps. "Just shut up and leave me alone!"

Then she was gone, while I was left behind, holding on to the fence, hating myself. Not only did this disastrous failure with Martha fill me with self-hate, but it reminded me that there was one more person I simply had to talk to.

From one until three o'clock, the time crawled by on centipede feet, moving fast but going nowhere. As I waited, I watched my classmates, who had spent lunch hour bunching up to talk to Penny, already beginning to drift away and avoid her. They didn't seem to like the fact that *she* was the one responsible for Harrington's sudden, unwelcome leave of absence. I should have felt good seeing that, but I didn't.

The only good thing was that now that Penny had short hair and feathered ears, we no longer looked alike. It had been the *hair*—just the heavy, swinging black hair that had made us so similar. Now most of hers was chopped off, matted up and sitting in some beauty-parlor trash can, about to be hauled off to the city dump. That thought was about the only cheering one I had as I dragged through the afternoon.

Then, at last, the 3:10 bell rang. Instead of leaving, however, I took myself to the sticky-walled, pure white yard bathroom marked *Girls*. There I perched on the sink, straining to look out of the little high-up window as Penny and all the others drifted out of school and took off in various directions. Penny was alone. All alone. Penny, Penny, Penny. I wondered where she was going and if she felt an ache inside the way I did. Some crazy part of me even wanted to run out after her and offer her comfort. But I didn't do it. I just sat there until the yard was empty except for the usual few boys shooting baskets. And still I didn't move. I was waiting.

Finally, juggling a lantern, a camp stove, and a box of books, Harrington came out of his building and headed toward his two-toned Chevy. That was my signal. I burst out of the bathroom, streaked across the street, and managed to fling one of the car doors open for him.

"Pru!" he said, startled by my sudden appearance.

"I wanted to say I'm sorry," I told him breathlessly, before he had a chance to say another word to me. "I say 'I'm sorry' a lot, and sometimes it annoys people, but I *am*—I *am* for all the mess and trouble I've made! I told Martha the same thing. She didn't want to listen, but I told her anyway. And I am sorry! So sorry for all the terrible trouble I've caused for both of you. Words don't help, I know—I know. But I've got to say them. Say them anyway even if they don't help. . . ."

Nodding and looking down at me, Ronald Harrington leaned his belongings against the front fender—the same one Penny and I had sat on, together, so many times. Then he spoke.

"You were on the roof," he said in a voice that sounded very tired. "It was Penny Hoffman on the fire escape, and Penny who spread all that nonsense to Cal Williams, making him swear to tell everybody it had been *you.* We questioned Cal yesterday and he told us. So, it was Penny mostly, and she will be dealt with. She's sick, I'm afraid. Mentally sick and she needs some kind of special . . . ."

"But I was there!" I cried out, simply unable to keep from interrupting. Hearing him call Penny sick scared me. Thinking about Penny and about her being sick and wondering if that made me sick, too, was horrible. "Being there—even on the roof and even if it wasn't my idea—was just as bad as being outside your window."

Mr. Harrington nodded. "So you feel full of guilt," he told me, shifting the stuff in his arms back onto the hood of the car so he didn't have to keep holding it. "All full of guilt."

"Yes," answered a small voice that appeared to be mine.

Rubbing at his beard, he leaned back against his fender. "All full of guilt," he mused. Then he repeated these same words over and over about a dozen times until I was so tired of hearing them I felt like hitting him. At last, however, he went on.

When he did, his voice had that terrible, passionate choked-up sound I'd heard twice before. In the men's bathroom at school and on my own front steps. "Sometimes, Pru—because words *can't* make up for deeds—people who hurt people end up punishing themselves.

Punishing and punishing as you are doing. Right? Now, do me a favor and run along, will you?"

Despite his words, I didn't move. For a minute I stood, trying to ignore the awful feeling in my stomach, as I stared at the things already packed into the back seat of his car. Then I spoke. "Where are you going?"

He shrugged. "Away. Camping. Away to be by myself. Now go on, will you? Go home."

I wanted to leave, but I couldn't. "Mr. Harrington?" I said.

"What, Pru?"

"Do you hate me? Hate me the way Martha does?"

Smiling in a slow-sad way that made wrinkles at the corners of his eyes, he shook his head. "No, although I'd like to. You richly deserve it. But, still, you do have . . . well, certain qualities about you, impressive ones that will be highly prized. You're different from Penny, Pru, you have a conscience and other qualities that will be greatly appreciated. . . ."

In the middle of this moving speech of his, I turned my back on him and started to run. He was standing there on the sidewalk telling me the same things he'd told Martha Brandeberry, but I wasn't going to stick around to listen.

"Pru!" he called out after me. "I was still talking to you. Where are you going?"

"Home!" I yelled back, pausing halfway down the block. "Like you told me to!"

"Without saying good-by?"

"Good-by!" I called, glad to be doing so at a comfortable distance. Glad just then that I'd never gotten to know more about Ronald B. Harrington, the True Man of Mystery. There was, after all, something creepy about a man who would let a sixth-grade nerd have a crush on him. Not at all romantic like the handsome heroes in the books I read. Not even worth what-iffing about. . . .

As I was telling myself these things, I heard him kick the door of his Chevy, making it slam. Then he muttered something I'd heard him say once before.

"Kids. I hate 'em!"

.15.

Maybe he hated kids and maybe he didn't. Suddenly I didn't care any more about Ronald Harrington's problems because I couldn't handle them. But there was something terribly important that I *could* handle right away. Not at home, though.

So without even stopping to think about it, I ran from Harrington's flat to the bus stop and caught the #38 to Civic Center. Next, I rushed between two sets of double glass doors and into the nearest elevator where I pressed the black button marked 27. Hardly a stomach-tumbling moment later, my feet hurried me out of the elevator, down a long echoing corridor, past an open-mouthed receptionist. Then, totally unannounced, I burst into my father's office.

He might have been holding an important meeting at that very moment, but he wasn't. Instead, he was sitting at his desk with his feet propped on the windowsill as he stared out at the smogless skyline of a windy blue day. He wasn't even pretending to be busy. He was just sitting there doing nothing.

When I flung myself into the room, he didn't turn around as if he was surprised either. He just said my name.

"Pru?"

"Huh?" I answered, wondering how my out-of-breath panting could be so distinctive that he knew it was me. Then I realized he didn't have to be any genius because the combination of afternoon sun and corner windows was floating reflected images of me right before his eyes.

"Well . . . what are you going to do?" he asked, addressing my shiny reflections instead of me.

"About what?" I asked, still struggling to catch my breath.

"About Penny Hoffman?"

He was continuing to stare at my window-images but also—at the same time—he was staring through them at the city rooftops while I was slumping back against his door, trying to remember clearly why it had been so important for me to come.

"She—Penny—she's not my friend any more," I told him as I began to pull myself together.

The minute I said that, his feet clopped to the floor and his squeaking chair swiveled around so that he was facing me. "It's just like that, is it? That simple. She's not your friend—so we'll take her and throw her out with the garbage?"

"But, Daddy, she's not my *friend* any more. She's bad. Like you said—with her I was only as good as my last . . . ."

"So we throw her out with the garbage. Just pitch her out. Isn't there anything about Penny worth saving?"

I didn't like the way this whole conversation was getting started. Somehow my father was saying the things *I* was supposed to be saying, and I was saying the things I had expected *him* to say.

He wasn't finished either. ". . . so because you were weak and let her lead you into trouble—serious trouble with Martha Brandeberry and Mr. . . . ."

"You know?" I gasped.

Solemnly, he nodded. "Of course, Pru. We've talked to everyone at school, your mom and I—a dozen times in the last two days. Do you think we're stupid or blind? Or that we'd just sit back and do nothing when our daughter is upset enough to try to pull earrings out of her ears without unscrewing them?"

"But, Daddy . . . ," I protested, wishing I could throw myself into his lap and cuddle there. I didn't do it, though. If that's what I'd really wanted, I would have run home where my mother—no questions asked —would have wrapped me in her arms.

Furrows deep enough to plant petunia seeds were lined up across my father's forehead. His voice, when he spoke again, sounded impatient. "Why did you come, Pru? Why did you fly in here to interrupt me in the middle of a busy day?"

For a moment I almost thought he was joking, since I had seen him doing absolutely nothing as I rushed in. Unless . . . he'd been busy brooding about me and about Penny.

"She's not going to be my friend again," I told him, reaching up to touch one of my wounded ears, ". . . but . . . ."

"But?" he repeated, leaning forward encouragingly.

"Yes. Yes. I guess there are things in her worth saving. But, Daddy . . . ."

"What, Pru?"

"You said before that there was something wrong with her. And today Mr. Harrington said it. Being cruel like she is—that isn't all normal, is it? And it's not just that she lies, it's the *kind* of lies. . . ."

"Is that why you came?" he asked. "To tell me something I already knew? To tell me that Penny's sick?"

There was no fussing around with him. He was sitting there looking through me as if I was a half-assembled Visible Dog Kit.

"Yes," I said, knowing that the time had come for me to stop stalling. "I came to tell you that. But I also came to see if *something can be done.*"

"For Penny?" my father asked, speaking very distinctly.

"Yes."

As he listened to my answer, he leaned back in his chair. Then, tapping a pencil against his knee and allowing his face—finally—to soften, he answered me. "I'm glad you're here. Glad you feel you can count on us. And, Pru, I think you're right, so your mom and I will see what we can do. I don't know what. It's a difficult problem. I can't make any promises that Penny or her family will listen. Or that treatment will make a difference. But we'll see. . . ."

Then for a long time, he didn't say anything. Neither did I. We just faced each other, listening to the sound of our own breathing. When he did speak again, his voice was low, so low I had to lean forward to hear.

"Help or no help, Pru—she'll be back. When this trouble blows over, she'll bounce back as beguiling as ever, pleading with you, charming you. How strong are you? What happens then?"

"I don't know," I answered, speaking very softly myself. "But what I want . . . I think . . . is not to *be* or *be with* the kind of person who hurts people. Penny mustn't be thrown out with the garbage, Daddy, but *I* don't need her. At least, I don't think I do. . . ."

As for the rest of what I had to say, I'm not sure whether I said it out loud or not, although I do remember leaving my father's office alone, catching the bus while I was still thinking and still talking.

". . . because," I was telling Daddy or myself or the seedy man dozing on the green vinyl seat next to me, "I don't need her or any other bossy, too close, silly-acting best friend who won't let me be me. . . ."

While I was saying these things, the bus made an extra-long stop at Fillmore Street. There, as I peered out the window, I saw a stranger sitting on top of a mailbox staring off into space. It was someone about my age with windblown hair, jeans, a sweatshirt, and a frowning face. I couldn't quite tell, though, whether I was looking at an unhappy boy or an unhappy girl.

I recognized that look, of course. I'd worn it often

enough myself when I sat around what-iffing. But to-day it bothered me to see it on someone else. In fact, it bothered me so much that, as the bus was beginning to pull away, I flung myself into an empty seat near an open window.

"Hey!" I called, sticking my head out and waving. "Hey, you there! Hi! Hi! Hey, listen—yes, *you*—on the mailbox. Hi! Hello! Hello-o-o!"

Something about my attitude must have been catch-ing because suddenly the person I was shouting at was standing up grinning instead of frowning, and wav-ing after me—wildly—with both arms.

Well . . . , I decided, as I kept on flapping my hand at the shrinking stranger on the mailbox, *a friend* might be okay. If it's just a *friend-friend.* A girl—or even a boy, maybe. . . .

"Hello-o-o!" I shouted again, knowing my voice couldn't still be heard back at Fillmore. But by now I was only yelling because I felt like it.

"Hello-o-o! Hello-o-o! Hello-o-o!"

Books by Susan Terris

TWO P'S IN A POD
(Greenwillow)

THE PENCIL FAMILIES
(Greenwillow)

THE CHICKEN POX PAPERS
(Franklin Watts)

NO BOYS ALLOWED
(Doubleday)

WHIRLING RAINBOWS
(Doubleday)

PLAGUE OF FROGS
(Doubleday)

PICKLE
(Four Winds Press)

THE DROWNING BOY
(Doubleday)

ON FIRE
(Doubleday)

AMANDA, THE PANDA, AND THE REDHEAD
(Doubleday)

THE BACKWARDS BOOTS
(Doubleday)

THE UPSTAIRS WITCH AND
THE DOWNSTAIRS WITCH
(Doubleday)